Adventure Alaska!
Stories For Boys

By Katy Kerris

Illustrated by Mineko Hummel & Matthew Eidem

Signed by the author.

Adventure Alaska! Stories For Boys

Library of Congress Control Number: 2009925476

ISBN: 978-1-57833-447-6

First Printing April, 2009

Printed in U.S.A.
through **Alaska Print Brokers**

Book layout and cover design: Vered R. Mares,
Todd Communications
Front Cover Illustration: Mineko Hummel
Back Cover Illustration: Matthew Eidem
Text Illustrations as follows:
Mineko Hummel Pages 8, 31, 32, 47, 94, 127
Matthew Eidem Pages 14, 15, 20, 41, 56, 62, 70-71,
81, 116

This book was typeset in 12 point Warnock Pro.

Published by
Adventure Alaska Publishing Co.
Anchorage, Alaska

Distributed by
Todd Communications
611 E. 12th Ave.
Anchorage, Alaska 99501-4603
(907) 274-8633 (TODD) Fax: (907) 929-5550
with other offices in Ketchikan, Juneau, Fairbanks and Nome Alaska
sales@toddcom.com • **WWW.ALASKABOOKSANDCALENDARS.COM**

List of Adventures

The Fish that Almost Got Away 4
Emory 10
Second Chance. 16
The Fog 22
Reconciliation. 28
Salmon King 33
I Love Gore 39
Monster 44
A Whale of a Tail 51
For the Love of Dogs. 60
Hanging in There 68
Bear Attack 79
Up a Creek without a Paddle 88
Alaska Grown. 97
Bloody Extra Toughs. 107
Avalanche 114
Never Sled with a Two Year Old 121

The Fish that Almost Got Away

A "bob" is a one-wheeled gear holder towed behind a bike. It attaches to the axle of the bike.

"There's no way we'll be able to go fishing," Dad says after talking to the park ranger. "A rock slide has closed the road to cars. Only four-wheelers are getting through."

"Rob has an idea," my younger brother Tyler says. "Bikes and a bob."

Dad looks at us, jaws open wide enough to ride a bike through.

"I'll tow the bob for any fish we catch and Tyler will carry the net," I explain.

"The extension net is fifteen feet long and it's five miles down a rutted, rocky road to our favorite fishing hole." Dad points to the road, which looks more like a trail. "Your mom will never agree."

"She says it's okay if we wear our helmets." I really want to go fishing. It's bad luck to go back home empty handed.

Dad knows when he's lost an argument. "Be back by two and be careful."

Tyler and I pack our fishing gear onto the bob and attach it by pin to the rear axle of my bike. The Copper River dip net fishery is one of Alaska's treasures. Each year millions of red and king salmon swim from the ocean upriver to their spawning grounds. Each year we drive 250 miles to catch our limit of 15 fish apiece. If we're lucky.

The bob and our daypacks are packed and we're ready to go. Tyler grabs the net, laying it diagonally across his shoulder and the handlebars. We start on the most hare-brained fishing trip imaginable.

"This net is hard to carry while biking," Tyler says, choking on a dust cloud left by a passing four-wheeler.

"Quit complaining and keep peddling," I say as I dodge a rock the size of a VW Beetle and crest a hill, making a mental note to avoid this on the way back. My teeth clank together as the bike, the bob and I careen down the hill. Tyler passes me as I barely make the turn at the bottom. "Where's the net?"

Tyler gestures behind. "The tree grabbed it on the way down."

It takes us fifteen minutes to untangle the net from the wily cottonwood tree. In that time at least twenty mosquitoes feast on my face. "Where's the insect repellant?"

"I thought Mom gave it to you."

"If we pedal fast enough they can't catch us," I say. "Hold onto the net this time."

It takes us over an hour to reach our fishing hole with the rolling, rutted road and our paraphernalia.

"What're we gonna do with all our fish?" Tyler asks. "The bob will only hold so many."

"Don't worry. We can hitch a ride back. Someone will take pity on us."

We hide our bikes in the trees and inch down the steep slope toward the river. Tyler trips on a tree limb and the next thing I know I'm looking up at the blue sky through netting, a welt forming on my forehead.

"Get me out," I yell.

Tyler's bent in two, laughing. "I caught a big one."

"I'm carrying the net the rest of the way," I growl.

We find the cluster of rocks we stand on to fish. I look into the brown, eddying and churned up water. Other fishermen are in the area, some tied off with rope to trees. Our rock is level and safe. Tyler and I have rock climbing training and we tie off the net with climbing rope.

Tyler takes the first shift wielding the net and I slap away at mosquitoes. "What's wrong with your nose?" he asks.

"A horde of mosquitoes just took off with it. My turn at the net." Tyler doesn't appear to be as bothered by the bugs.

Later my arms are aching from holding the net in the strong current and it starts to rain. The mosquitoes go into hiding but the rocks become slick.

"I'd be better off in my hockey skates," Tyler says.

I pull the safety rope off the net and rope up Tyler instead. "Maybe we should go back," he says. He looks like a drowned rat with chicken pox.

"Not empty handed." Fishing is slow but guys around us are pulling them in.

An hour later we have one red salmon to our name. "We're not empty handed," Tyler announces.

I can tell he wants to go back. It's stopped raining and the bugs are back. We pack the gear and carry our one fish to the trail. A guy toting a 20 pound king salmon approaches. "I've been watching you young men and I want to give you this."

"No thanks," "Okay!" Tyler and I both say together.

Tyler turns to me. "I want the fish. It's as good as catching our own."

"Okay, but you have to carry it."

Tyler grasps the monster from the stranger. "Thanks, sir. It's been a slow day." Tyler caresses the slimy head of the salmon. "It's a beautiful fish, Rob."

I roll my eyes.

Lugging the lunker up the hill is no easy task. I have to help Ty or we'll never make it back. We're sweating and covered with leaves and dirt by the time we get to the bikes.

I squat to attach the two fish to the bob. The tail of the king hangs over the edge. "Be careful with it," Tyler says.

"You're awfully attached to this fish," I reply, completing the job.

It's an uneventful trip back to the parking area until the last hill. I go first, my arms taking the brunt of the jostling. Then I hit the VW rock. I fly up off the seat, barely hanging on. I hear something approaching fast on the left. I get a glimpse of the king salmon, eyes and mouth open wide passing me, riding the bob. He's screaming "No!!!"

Tyler's mouth is open too as he passes me without the net, hot on the fish's tail. The bob hits another rock and now it's a flying fish.

Tyler and I apply the brakes and start locating gear strewn all over the place. I finally catch up to the salmon which I swear is trying to slither down to the river.

Eventually we drag into the parking lot. I've never been so happy to see Mom and Dad.

"What happened to your fish?" Dad says, lifting the bruised, dirt and leaf-covered salmon off the bob.

"This is nothing. You should have seen the ones that got away."

Emory

Emu are flightless birds native to Australia. They can reach 6'5" in height and can sprint 30 mph.

"I need a puppy," I announced one day to Mom. "We need a puppy like we need a hole in the head."

"Everyone has a puppy."

"Do I detect a hint of whining in your voice? You know how I adore whining." Mom rolled her eyes at that point. "Everyone has a puppy," she mimicked in a voice creepily familiar.

That was three years ago. We never got a puppy but we did get an egg. A really big egg. A gigantic egg.

My younger brother Tyler and I came home from school. He went immediately to the fridge to feed his bottomless pit.

"There is absolutely nothing to eat," he said, rummaging around.

"An egg," I said, pointing. The egg was in a laundry basket surrounded by towels with a light bulb close to it. It was the size of an oblong cantaloupe.

"I hate eggs. You know that. The rubbery white part freaks me out."

"I've never seen such a giant egg." I reached out to touch it.

Tyler emerged from the fridge with some jelly, mayo and an apple, and then grabbed the pickles off the shelf.

"Tell me you're not eating that together."

"What in the world..." Tyler said, spotting the egg. The pickles and the mayo hit the floor and the resulting mess was about the size of Delaware.

"That's really disgusting," I said, leaving the room.

Several days later the egg cracked and out came the ugliest creature I've ever seen.

"It's an emu," Mom said, eyes aglow. "We'll call him Emory."

"'Ugly' would be a better name," I whispered to Tyler.

"Or 'Hideous'."

"Jesse just got a puppy," I said.

"Let's go play with a real pet."

Mom heard that comment. Perhaps she'd heard them all. "You'll be the first in the neighborhood to have an emu as a pet."

"It is *not* my pet."

Emory grew quickly and looked like a small, gray and black shaggy ostrich, which is to say he was never very handsome. He followed us around like humans were his mama. He had the habit of butting us with his head and short, stiff beak wherever he could reach.

One day he kept hitting me, well, in the butt.

"Isn't that cute," Mom said.

"Stay away, you pervert." I pushed Emory's head away.

Tyler snickered from the couch. "Dare you to take Emory for a walk."

"That would be nice." Mom got a faraway look in her eye. I hate it when she gets that look. It means she's thinking.

The next day she handed me a long leash. "What's this for?" I asked.

"To walk Emory. Look how much he wants to go outside."

Emory as usual was standing by her side.

"People walk puppies, not emus."

"I've got your favorite dinner cooking."

"Can't resist that, Rob," Tyler said from behind Mom. "Be a sport and take our pet for a walk."

"Out, Mister," Mom said, grabbing Tyler by the ear. "You're going too."

Emory hated the leash. With the halter-style leash on his sleek black feathers he refused to move. He stuck out his tongue like he was choking.

"You're hurting him," Tyler said once we were in the yard.

"You do it, then." I threw the leash on the ground and stalked away. "I wanted a puppy."

Three houses later, something tapped me on the back. "Leave me alone, Ty." I pushed him away. The tapping continued, and I pushed him away again. Finally I turned around to apply a disabling punch and came face to face with Emory, dragging his leash.

By now it was covered in leaves, grass, and good old Alaskan mud. I took the leash off. Apparently Emory would follow without it.

Soon Emory was the talk of the neighborhood and everyone wanted to come over and see him.

"Told you so," Mom said. I hate it when she's right.

Emory played football with us, chased away stray dogs, and scared the crap out of Lester the Loser Cat from down the street. It's safe to say Lester will never leave presents for us to clean up anymore. Not only that, Emory was the best mouse catcher on the street, chasing the poor little buggers down and eating them with one snap of his beak.

"You have the most awesome pet," kids would say. "Can I touch him?"

"He has teeth the size of my fingers," I'd say, watching the hands go back in the pockets.

Tiffany, the cutest girl on the street, began hanging out every day after school.

"I love animals. I want to be a vet." She stooped to examine Emory's feet. "I've never seen anything with three toes before. Sort of like a dinosaur."

"They're called 'tridactyl' toes," Ty announced. The nerd had done his research on emu.

"I think she's in love with me," I confided to Tyler.

"Wipe that silly look off your face. She's in love with our Emory."

"Emory is *my* emu," I said, scratching the short, prickly feathers on the head now as tall as my own.

"*Our* emu." Tyler straightened the feathers on his back. Emory closed his eyes and lapped up the attention.

Emory loved our backyard. When he got too big for the house he'd be out there all the time, pecking around for food, stalking the fenced perimeter. The magpies loved him, or maybe his food, and always hung out near the fence by Emory. Tyler and I built him a lean-to so he'd have some protection from the rain.

One day in late fall I heard a scream from the kitchen. "Emory!" There was the sound of a shattering dish. "Get away, you beast!"

I hurried to the window in time to see a magnificent grizzly, its golden brown fur ruffled by the wind, climbing over the fence like it was nothing.

"Rob, do something!" Mom was beside herself and looked like she was going to lunge out the door and throw herself between the bear and Emory.

Before I could grab the shotgun, the most amazing thing I've ever seen happened. Emory charged that bear.

Now bears can run really fast, at least 30 mph. But Emory was much faster and he was mad. There was an intruder in his yard! Emory chased that griz all around our yard. The griz's ears were back and he looked as scared as a sinner who's seen his death. I've never seen eyes that big on a grizzly. Maybe he was looking for an escape route as he took two laps around the yard. Finally he jumped over the fence, Emory nipping him on the butt and clacking his beak.

Mom was out there in a flash and I followed with the gun.

"You brave, brave emu," she chortled, patting Emory's head.

"That was something, wasn't it Rob?" I think she was crying.

I nodded. I was speechless. My emu had just chased away the biggest griz I'd seen in Anchorage. And to think I wanted a puppy.

Second Chance

Sitka black-tailed deer are smaller than other American deer. Kodiak brown bear are plentiful on the island and are the largest bears in the world, reaching 1500 pounds.

Thwap! Another green-fletched arrow hits the bull's eye. I pull down my bow.

"Three in a row. A chip off the old block," Dad says, coming up behind.

Dad is one of the best local bow hunters here on Kodiak Island. Aside from deer, he's taken grizzly with a bow. Pictures of Dad and his kills litter the walls of our house.

I feel my chest swell with pride. "I think I'm ready for our hunt."

Dad claps his calloused hand on my shoulders, now broadened and firm after a summer as deckhand on a fishing boat. "Tomorrow morning, bright and early, Ryan. Pack for an overnight trip."

I'm not an early riser, but this morning I'm awake before the alarm. Outside it's typical Kodiak fall weather—cool and cloudy with a steady rain, the kind that won't let up all day. I layer my polypro and wool as chill is the death of someone in the wilderness.

"Perfect weather for a hunt," Dad says. "Still up for it?"

I nod. I've been waiting for this day all summer.

We load our old pick-up with all our gear and drive to the harbor. "I've got the perfect spot in mind." Dad starts the motor on our 23-foot Alumaweld. "We'll have it to ourselves and guaranteed to see deer."

We motor out of the harbor and across the bay, grateful to be inside the cabin of the boat as the windshield wipers swat the rain. I've always loved the sea and been comfortable out on the swells. It seems almost home to me.

"Part kelpie, you are Ryan," Mom always used to say. "It's your Irish blood, from your Dad's side." I swallow hard. Mom's death three years ago still sits heavy on me.

"Thinking of your mom?"

I shrug. Dad can always tell. "Thinking of the hunt."

He nods. I suspect he knows the truth. "Every hunt is a great hunt."

We anchor in a cove. Dad lowers a small Zodiak into the water and we climb in with our gear. We put to shore and Dad ties her up so the tides don't take her away. "It'd be a cold swim to the boat."

Cold and deadly. The sea's what got Mom. I focus on double checking my pack.

"Ready?"

I follow Dad through the thick woods. We pass quietly, trying not to disturb branches and leaves, our footsteps muffled by the thick fern and moss ground cover and the soft sound of rain in the branches overhead. The fir and pine needles whisper in the light breeze. At times Dad, in his camouflage, is barely visible up ahead. If I unfocus my eyes he blends right in.

Dad pauses and in a fluid movement, notches an arrow and lets it fly. He follows with a second. We both move forward and he stoops to lift two dead spruce hens, heads lolling to the side on plump bodies.

He motions to the left. "More. Go on. I'll wait."

I scan the forest floor for movement and see it out of the corner of my eye. I have an arrow in my hand before I can think, aim, and let fly. My aim is true. It's a clean kill and I retrieve the limp bird, removing my arrow. Dad stows my bird in his backpack with the other two.

We walk in silence but see nothing more than a red squirrel. She chatters a warning in her loud voice as we pass.

Finally we get to an open area. "We'll camp here. There is bear sign but it isn't fresh and at least nothing will surprise us."

Dad removes his pack and places his rifle nearby. Though we are hunting with bow and arrow, a rifle is an important safety measure against the huge Kodiak grizzlies so common here.

We put up the tent and light a fire that doesn't burn well because of the dampness of the wood. Dad prepares the birds and places them in foil in the fire.

"Nothing's better than fresh spruce hen." We both lick the grease off our fingers.

After dinner we sit around the smoking fire. "I always think about your mom in the evenings. It's when I miss her most."

I nod.

"The native Aleuts believe an ancestor never leaves a loved one. They stay and help the living."

"Mom was part Aleut."

Dad nods. "She was proud of her Native heritage."

As we climb into the tent I have a lot to think about, not the least of which is our hunt tomorrow morning.

* * * * *

In the morning, Dad is lead again in the misty rain. "There's a meadow up ahead. Should be deer."

Dad hands me the binoculars and I scan the meadow.

"On the far side. A huge buck and several does, grazing on grass."

I look again. "They really blend in."

Dad nods. "Nature's way. It's what helps them survive against predators. That and speed, and this group can fly like the wind if they hear or see us. We'll skirt the meadow under the trees."

He doesn't have to tell me to be quiet. It takes some time to creep along, as careful as we are not to spook the herd. As luck would have it, they are moving in our direction and we're downwind.

"Fifty yards from the buck now," Dad whispers. "One of the largest I've seen."

He is magnificent, all rippling muscle and tawny color.

"You take the shot. Use all the cover you can to get closer. Take your time. You'll probably only get one shot before they bolt."

I nod and visually plan my route before starting. My stomach's doing somersaults. My first deer! It is a moment I've been waiting for since I was a little kid watching Dad go hunting.

I creep along, foot by foot, sometimes ducking behind a bush on all fours. Finally I know I'm close enough to take a shot. I carefully reach for and notch an arrow, soundless.

I hear the buck chewing grass; see drops of water drip from his antlers. I hope he can't hear my heart thudding in my chest. It seems deafening to me, but the buck grazes on. I draw back my arrow, the area just behind his left foreleg dead in my sights.

Suddenly he lifts his head and sniffs the breeze. And I smell the wet grass and the nearness of the does. I see out of his liquid brown eyes the tall trees of his forest, and hear the waterfall I hadn't noticed with my own ears. I feel his muscles ripple powerfully under his skin. I am magnificent. I am King.

Water drips from my hat and onto my hand, at the ready. All I have to do is let fly and he's mine.

"Ryan." It's Mom's voice clear as day. "Left, Ryan."

I swivel my head left to see a massive grizzly stalking me at 20 feet. I swing my bow around and let fly. He screams as my arrow hits him in the shoulder as he lunges forward. I hear the sharp echo of two rifle shots and the bear crumples at my feet as the buck takes off with a powerful leap. The entire harem disappears into the wispy mist, vanishing like ghosts.

Dad approaches at a run and unloads another round into the grizzly to make sure he's good and dead. We're both stunned as we think about what almost happened. "You got away a nice shot, Son."

I nod. "Next time we'll get the deer." As I say it, I don't know if I'll hunt deer again. The feeling of being the buck is still powerful in me, as is the fear of being prey to a larger animal. I feel something warm trickle down my cheek. Maybe it is a raindrop.

After dressing out the grizzly, we make our way back to the boat. Mom's presence is still with me, too. I believe she saved my life. She gave me a second chance.

The Fog

There are many tribes of Alaskan Natives. The Tlingit (pronounced "Klin-ket") live in Southeastern Alaska.

Jeremy unzipped his tent fly and stepped out into a brilliant day. He squinted as he glanced at the sun already cresting the mountains around Glacier Bay.

His favorite place in the world, and the weather the best he'd seen this year.

This year—the first of his 17 years Mom and Dad allowed him to go kayaking by himself for a week. His younger brother, James, had been dying to come along. But Jeremy had refused. It was like a coming of age trip for him, reflecting his Native Alaskan Tlingit heritage and independence. He felt like the luckiest person alive.

The sun reflected off something near the shoreline. The object drew him like a magnet. Jeremy squatted and picked up a perfectly intact metallic Thermos, like his own. Shaking it, he heard something inside, so he opened it. A whiff of hot chocolate hit his nose, but the liquid had not made the noise. He reached in with two fingers and pulled out a folded piece of paper.

Was that a smear of blood along the edge, or hot chocolate?

Jeremy shivered, despite the warmth of the sun over his shoulder, and the gentle lapping of water on the rocks of his crescent-shaped beach.

Surely nothing important. But why shove a note in a Thermos and set it out to sea? The remnants of hot chocolate seemed fresh and even lukewarm.

Jeremy opened the note and read the spidery, shaky writing which trailed off at the end. "It's here. It's here again and I can't get away. It has sucked the life out of everything. The world is cold, so cold …"

What was "it" anyway? Jeremy turned the paper over but saw nothing to answer his questions. He felt something watching him and turned abruptly toward his tent. Nothing but a camp robber bird, looking for leftovers near his fire pit.

Suddenly he knew he had to leave. The Thermos slid from his nerveless fingers and clattered onto the rocks of the beach. The skin between his shoulder blades tingled. It's nothing, he kept telling himself. Someone playing a prank. What could happen on this beautiful day in his favorite place?

As he struck his tent and packed his dry bags he couldn't shake a growing sense of panic. The marine radio monotoned surrounding weather conditions as perfect July weather as one could have in Southeastern Alaska. Even the forecast sounded good.

Jeremy untied his kayak and dragged it to the shoreline, then began stuffing the hatches with gear. Two days from home, but with an early start and the tide moving with him, maybe he could make it by dark. He yearned for home like he never had.

Again his skin prickled and he turned to look over his shoulder. Nothing. A drop of sweat trickled down his back. He shivered. It felt ten degrees cooler. He breathed into the air and saw the steam of his breath. Jeremy checked his portable weather station. It read 65 F. He slapped the machine and checked again. 65 F it stubbornly persisted.

Goosebumps rose on his skin. Now he was just paranoid. He pulled his lifejacket on and stepped into his spray skirt. Climbing carefully into his cockpit, he shoved off from shore and snapped the skirt around for protection from the water. This was usually his most favorite part of the day—the whole world at his feet and who knew what he might see or discover. But today had no joy, no matter how hard he tried to concentrate on the positives.

Something was floating on the water ahead. Paddle on by, don't look, he told himself. But he was drawn to the item—a kayak paddle, fully assembled and not in any way harmed. It could be brand new. He didn't touch it, paddling hard right by.

No one loses a paddle, unless...

What was on the horizon now? Jeremy removed his shades and rubbed his eyes, looking again. Was that fog along the surface of the water? Fog wasn't uncommon in the area, and he had paddled in it before, but something about the unexpectedness of this fog on such a sunny day freaked him out.

He paddled closer to shore so he could land if needed and wait it out. But the fog was rolling toward him much faster than natural. He knew where the shore should be, but it became obscured before he could reach it. Soon he was enveloped in it, a part of it, and cut off from everything: the sun, the shore, any noise but the sound of his paddle strokes hitting the water.

It was damp and cool, so much so that the sweat from his exertion chilled him to the bone. He unsnapped his spray skirt and threw his emergency rain gear over himself, life vest and all.

It was eerily still, and he was afraid. He felt his pulse pounding in his ear. The water was flat steely gray without a ripple. He could see nothing but white in every direction. His breath fogged around him. His weather station showed it had dropped 20 degrees. In 30 minutes? He fumbled with cold fingers in his safety bag for the radio. Nothing but static. The weather report could always be heard! He felt for his compass. The needle swung crazily from side to side. A sense of doom blanketed him like the fog. What the hell was happening?

He could make out something large floating in the water ahead. He knew he didn't want to see it, but shutting his eyes was out of the question. He didn't have to move a muscle as the object drifted toward him. It was a ghostly kayak, upside-down. Its bow tapped his boat as it glided soundlessly by.

Jeremy began paddling with all his might but noticed even in his frenzy his paddle strokes were eerily silent. In the featureless world he had no bearings, nothing to tell him if he was making progress. Time never lied. He paused to look at this watch. It had stopped at 9:35, the minute he entered the fog!

He was shivering uncontrollably now. He had to get to shore, start a fire and warm up. At the least, crawl into his sleeping bag.

Jeremy guessed at the direction of shore and began paddling. He stopped in incredulity. His paddle strokes no longer made circular ripples in the water. His rudder produced no wake to prove his passing. He rubbed his eyes and looked again. Nothing.

His bow thudded against something he hadn't seen. The kayak again! This time, it was trailing a blue jacket that looked familiar. Jeremy picked at his own jacket. They were identical down to the small tear on the left sleeve.

"No! No! No!" he yelled into the fog to each stroke of his paddle. He needed to keep paddling or he was a goner.

He never hit shore. He never saw anything else in the fog. He was exhausted and stopped paddling. His long hair clung to the sides of his face and he felt unexplained warmth suffuse his body. He removed his jacket and tucked it into the bungees on his kayak deck.

He had no idea how long he'd been paddling or where he was. He found he didn't care anymore.

Once again the strange kayak approached his boat and bobbed against his bow. He knew what he had to do. As he leaned forward to grasp the hull of the boat his own paddle fell into the water and floated away. A ghostly figure, clothing ballooned out, parted from the kayak, descending slowly into the colorless water.

Jeremy knew what he would find when he turned the boat over. He heard a voice as if from a distance intoning words from a childhood story. *"Made cold by the world."*

Reconciliation

Raven plays a big part in Alaskan native legend, often working with the People to solve problems in everyday life.

James stood at the bow of the motor boat, reveling in the feeling of the cold wind tearing at his jet black hair, tied back in an old rubber band to keep it under control. His dad drove the boat, and his mom and younger sister hunkered behind the console, out of the wind and the misty rain.

James loved being out in Glacier Bay. His Tlingit ancestors had lived in this area since before time was measured, and it was a part of his heritage, his blood, his birthright. He didn't even feel the drops of rain slashing across his face, or feel chilled in the cool wind.

A raven croaked as it flew over the boat, turning a beady black eye on the occupants as if he owned this bay they traveled in. Raven had supernatural powers in Tlingit legend and James couldn't help but wonder— had his brother Jeremy been visited by this very raven on his disastrous trip several weeks before? Family and friends were still in shock over Jeremy's disappearance. A massive search of the entire area found nothing but his overturned kayak floating, empty. Every boat in their town of Gustavus had looked for Jeremy, along with the Coast Guard. Finally the searchers had to admit that Jeremy, even with his many years of kayaking experience, had stumbled into some kind of trouble and drowned.

The boat slowed as it approached a rocky, crescent-shaped beach lined with spruce and fir. This, an ideal kayaker's beach, may have appealed to Jeremy as well.

"We'll camp here tonight," James's dad said. He had uttered few words since his oldest son's disappearance.

James missed Jeremy terribly. Jeremy was the stronger, wiser, braver son of his parents, and stubbornly like his dad. James knew he could never physically match Jeremy in tasks like cutting firewood and pulling struggling salmon out of a set net. "Look out, Little Brother" seemed to be Jeremy's favorite saying, followed by his deep, warm laugh.

"You put up the tents." His dad threw the tents across the beach in James's direction, and they slipped through his arms and clattered onto the stones beneath.

James struggled to put the poles together and attach the tent flies in a gusty wind. Still, no one helped him. "Let me help you with that Little Brother." He could almost hear Jeremy's voice on the wind. James choked on a lump rising in this throat, and felt hot tears slide down his cheeks.

"Dinner!" his mom announced. James wiped at his wet cheeks. It wouldn't do to show his emotions now that he was the oldest son.

After a quiet dinner, James's father stoked the fire. "We are here this day to honor the memory of our son and brother Jeremy who was taken away from us before his time. Our Tradition believes the spirit of a person recently passed is still present for many days. I have felt Jeremy's presence since we entered this cove. Perhaps he will communicate with us throughout our trip."

At that moment a raven flew over, wedge-shaped tail ruddering in the wind, and making a noise sounding like two hollow stones tapped together.

Whatever his dad said next was lost on James. He was already thinking about what he might say to Jeremy, should he have a chance. These thoughts continued that night in his lonely tent. He didn't even bother to lay out his sleeping bag, and instead leaned his back against its rolled-up bulk watching summer's twilight deepen.

He must have fallen asleep because when he woke the rain had stopped. He stretched his stiff back. It was very early in the morning and no one else stirred in the camp. James sensed a change in the weather, and when he opened his tent he could see it was a clear morning, and the sun was beginning to rise over the mountains across the bay.

A raven appeared out of nowhere and plopped down on the beach in front of him, looking up with an intelligent eye. "What do you want?"

The raven said nothing, but leaped across the beach in big hops. James followed to a small creek of fresh water draining from the forest, across the rocks, into the bay. Here the raven stooped to drink. James remembered the words of an old shaman. "Invite a wandering spirit to visit with a basin of fresh water."

James wasn't sure exactly what to do, but he went back to camp and rummaged through the kitchen gear until he found a large frying pan. Returning to the creek, he filled it up with icy water, under the watchful eye of the raven. "Now what?" The raven tilted his head, looking at him with a knowing eye. "Since you've lost your voice, I'll have to make it up on my own."

At that moment, James felt the warming presence of the sun strike his back. A large, flat rock lay at his feet, so he turned toward the sun, sat down, and placed the pan on the rock. He looked into the water as the ripples calmed, and saw the sky and a fringe of spruce trees. As he looked a figure materialized and walked toward him. "Jeremy."

"Little Brother. It's good to see you."

James could not respond as he didn't trust his voice. Jeremy looked fit even if his lines and colors were a little wavery in the water.

"Don't cry. I'm fine here."

"I'm sorry, about fighting."

"Don't be sorry, Little Brother. You are always close to my heart."

James placed his hand on his heart. "And you."

"You will grow strong, marry, and have many children. A good life."

"I'll never forget you."

"Remember, then. It is good."

"Stay..."

"I can't stay, but I'll always be with you."

The sound of wing beats overhead and a deep "cro-ak, cro-ak" wrested James' attention from the pan. He watched the raven fly across the water and disappear into the forest beyond. When he looked back into the pan, the reflection was gone. But the feeling of his brother's presence stayed with him, a warm feeling, deep inside his being.

He dumped the pan of water and slowly walked back to the camp.

Salmon King

Pound for pound, red ("sockeye") salmon are one of the most powerful sport fish to catch. King ("Chinook") salmon can weigh up to 97 pounds in the Kenai River.

"Aren't you ready yet Rob?" Tyler asks. He's all geared up in his rubber hip waders, hat and the safety glasses Mom makes us wear when we're combat fishing on the Russian River. We call it combat fishing because it can be shoulder to shoulder, with eyeball-removing hooks flinging all over the place.

"I've gotta get this fly just right." I'm tying on my new Russian-River-catchamillion-fish fly I made over the winter.

"It looks pretty small." Ty looks doubtful.

"Looks can be deceiving. Reds don't bite anyway. The fish won't see this expertly tied bugger till it's eased into the jaw and Bam! I'll have it." I love my seven-weight fly rod in these waters. Light enough to feel each bump and flexible enough to get a real battle from these fighting fish.

Ty clutches his old rod and reel. "Grandpa's pole always gives me good luck."

"You'll need it, bro, if you're going to catch more than me tonight."

Ty taps his toe. "It's hard to catch fish from the parking lot."

"I'm coming." I stomp past a sign warning that grizzlies have been seen in the area.

The Kenai River fishery is one of the best known in the world and we line up along the banks with thousands of others from around Alaska and around the world. Solitude it isn't, but fun it is, especially when one of the determined salmon hits your line.

"Nothing better," I say as we climb down the stairway in the dusky light. The river sings sweetly as it rushes over rocks and tree roots. We like to come in the evenings and spend the night fishing to avoid the crowds. Mom and Dad are asleep in the campground.

"Careful of bears. Make a lot of noise and stay together," Mom said earlier, handing over the pepper spray bear deterrent. "And this time bring back fish, not just fish-y tales."

Ty and I looked at each other. We deserved it with the luck we've had this year. "It's fish in the freezer with these salmon-slaying flies," I believe I said.

Mom rolled her eyes and pushed us out the door.

Tyler hits the river first and starts working the water.

"The current's too fast here." I'm looking for a perfect spot, and I find one, wading out knee deep still within sight of Ty.

On my second cast I've got one. "Rob the Great!" The fish runs and pulls out line. I reel it in and out it goes again, arching my rod like a rainbow. Soon it's under control and I pull the pliers out of my back pocket and set the hen free. "Lay a lot of eggs, you lucky fish. And don't bite any more lures, especially his." I put one finger in the air. Ty turns away, but I know he's seen me expertly catch and release the fish.

The Alaskan night rolls on, never getting fully dark. I've lost count of the number of fish I've caught but have two big guys on my stringer. My line zips out again and I check my watch. 1:30 a.m. "I'm gonna keep this one and call it a night," I yell to Ty. I don't tell him I'm pretty tired. I swear Ty is part werewolf. He can stay up all night and never look sleepy the next day.

Ty walks over, dragging his stringer of two fish. "I still need one fish, Rob. We're not leaving yet. You promised and I know I can catch another one." He must see my indecision. "Please?"

"Take my lucky fly." I cut it off and hand it over.

Ty spends the next hour fishing without a hit. "It's all dried up, Rob."

"Let's go back."

"You promised; three fish."

"I didn't think it'd take you all night."

"A promise is a promise."

Ty walks down river some more. There's a group of fishermen ahead we can just make out in the twilight, at the confluence of the Russian and the Kenai Rivers. Ty wades in and I sit down on the bank, leaning against a log.

The next thing I hear is people screaming "Hey bear!" and pointing to me. A guy's got a gun and pushes his kid behind him.

"Rob! Look out!"

I scramble to my feet in time to see a grizzly eyeing my fish. I wave my arms and yell, grabbing my bear spray canister, and she retreats.

I feel a little shaky. "Just a young one anyway."

"She outweighs you by 300 pounds, Rob. Stay awake."

I move to another spot, one with a good view in every direction. "Thirty minutes and we're going."

Maybe I fall asleep again, but a cry from Ty wakens me. "Rob, help!"

His pole is bent double toward the water, at the mercy of a huge fish. I can't believe it hasn't snapped. He manages to hold the pole, but slips on a rock and is pulled in. I rush to help, but at that moment the griz reappears and snatches my stringer.

"Rob!" I want my fish back, but Ty is in trouble. I rush into the water and pull him up, sputtering, but still holding the rod. His two fish are attached to his stringer, attached to his belt.

"Come on, Ty, bring it in." I'm aware of a group of people watching.

"I'm trying. I think my rod's gonna break."

"Don't exaggerate. Tire it out until it's ready to come in."

At that moment, a huge king salmon porpoises out of the water and Ty's line zings taut. Ty loses his balance again fighting the behemoth. I lunge to grab him and my boot slips on his slimy fish and we're both in the water.

Ty somehow manages to hold on as we haul ourselves out. A small crowd has gathered to watch. "Must be tourists," one guy says.

Ty's doing a dance, chasing the fish upriver and downriver, slipping on rocks and the fish on his stringer. Every now and then the king bursts out of the water and runs toward the fast current.

"It's gotta be a 40-pounder," someone says.

Ty trips over his stringer line and bites it again. This time his rod flies out of his hand. I manage to snag it as it zips by. I'm sure the fish is gone with the slack introduced to the line, but amazingly it's still on as I haul the rod back.

Ty's trying to untangle himself from the stringer. A guy is helping him but the next thing I know his stringer is flowing past me. I try reaching for it but Ty yells "The king, Rob!"

He's at my elbow grabbing for the rod. By now his waders must be dangerously heavy with water. "It's my fish to land!"

I hand the rod back. I doubt grandfather's old rod will take this kind of beating and survive. Mine would've busted into a million pieces by now.

I stand close to Ty as he wrestles the monster to shore. Even with the exertion his teeth are chattering. Finally the big hog is at our feet. I lean to pull out the fly. "King's not legal here," I say.

"Get out your camera, Rob. We're getting a picture before we let him go."

Ty kneels next to the huge fish. I take out the soggy camera and snap a shot, and Ty releases the fish. We watch as it fins into the deeper current and is gone.

"Sun's coming up," Ty says.

I think the sky is getting lighter. After two in the morning, my watch says. I'm bone tired and feel like I've been wrestling in a match against three bigger guys.

Ty opens his mouth. "We're going back, Ty. We're both soaked. We'll be hypothermic any minute."

Ty lies down on the ground, lifts his feet into the air, and lets the water run out of the waders. He's shaking now. We gather our gear and make a beeline for the campground, empty-handed once again.

"I hope that bear's enjoying my fish."

"It was the best fishing trip ever," Ty says. "Show me the photo."

I take the camera out and turn it on. Nothing.

Ty looks at me. "Mom and Dad'll never believe us."

I can't believe we've done it again. No fish between the two of us.

"I'm changing and coming out again. New day, new limit." Ty has a gleam in his eye.

"Over Mom's dead body."

We're at the camper now. Ty rummages around in his bag for clothes, grabs a jar of peanut butter and a spoon without waking anyone.

"Got another lucky fly?"

I Love Gore

An adult has about 11 pints of blood. A person can lose up to 50% of their blood and still survive.

You know those movies with the gallons of blood redder than realistically possible, and swords running through a victim tied to the table? Limbs hacked off and blood spurting to the ceiling? Yep, that's what I do with my spare time. I dink around on the internet finding images I like and doctoring them with special effects. I've created some really great ones and put them right back out there. They get a lot of hits, too. One day I'll be a movie maker, if only I didn't live in dumb Alaska. I mean, seriously, are any of the great Hollywood film makers from Alaska? I dare you to name one.

Then something happened that changed my life.

My pal Jon and I and our dads took our machines up onto some of the frozen lakes up north. We have a small cabin there, about ten miles off the road. Snow machine or four-wheeler is the only way to get there, besides flying in on a float plane.

Anyway, we got up and had a big breakfast then spent the day racing our machines on the lakes. Afterward, Dad suggested Jon and I chop wood while he cooked dinner.

Jon's a big burly guy about twice my size so he offered to do the chopping. He sharpened the axe and rolled up his sleeves and looked like a regular Paul Bunyan. I kept him laughing about blood and guts and stories I'd read off the internet as he chopped.

"That photo you doctored of our teacher was great. The brains really looked like snakes. How'd you get it so real looking?"

"My secret. Getting a picture of her smiling was harder."

"How'd you get the blood to shoot out of her eyes?"

"Easy. I'll show you when we get home."

Carrying an armload of wood inside, I heard the sound of the axe hitting something that couldn't have been wood and heard Jon scream. There's nothing worse than hearing a man scream. The wood tumbled to the ground as I sprinted toward Jon. The sight of him stopped me dead in my tracks. Bright red blood was squirting all over the white snow.

"Help, Josh, I'm hit bad." Jon had his hand over his foot and still blood poured onto the snow and soaked his new snow pants.

I knew I should help, but I was paralyzed.

"Help!" Jon yelled, over and over.

Both Dads ran past me to Jon.

"Jon!" Mr. Clellan yelled. I knew what he meant. It was an awful lot of blood.

"He's split the shoe open. Keep the pressure on," Dad said.

"I saw the bone." Jon's Dad was panicked.

I still couldn't look. Jon's breathing was faster than a man's out to be.

"He'll hyper-ventilate. Slow breaths, Jon."

"I'm going to die!" Jon was flailing around with his arms, accidently pushing Dad away.

"Josh, run inside and cut the curtain into strips. Find a towel. Hurry!"

My legs finally moved. I could help as long as I didn't have to see. I did what he said and ran back

41

outside and handed the shredded curtain to Dad. His shirt was off and wadded up over the wound but a blood stain blossomed through the thick shirt.

"We're miles from help," Mr. Clellan said.

Dad still pressured the wound. "No phones out here. He may lose the foot. Or..."

Lose his foot or what? Die? The scene was as macabre as any grisly picture I'd seen. Blood was all over Jon, on the Dads' hands, and all over the pristine snow. So much nauseating blood—I couldn't believe he wasn't already a goner.

Suddenly it hit me. This was my best friend. Surely he wouldn't die.

Josh's face was pale and drawn. He was biting his lip. I've never seen Dad look so scared.

"Get a sleeping bag, Josh."

Dad and Mr.Clellan carried Jon to a sled. They loaded him on in front of his dad.

"Wrap the bag around him," Dad said. Jon was ghostly white.

"Where are we going? Dad?" Jon said. He seemed disoriented.

"I think there's a clinic in Healy, and phone service at the road," Dad said.

Jon and Mr. Clellan were gone as we got our machines started. We caught up with them halfway back to the truck. I helped hoist Jon onto the bench seat of the extended cab. Dad was on the phone talking to someone about Jon as he removed the snow machine trailer from the hitch.

"You sit with him." Mr. Clellan propped Jon's legs on one bag and covered him with another. "Keep him alert."

"Mom? Where's Mom?" Jon muttered.

"It's me, Josh. Hang on, buddy." It was the longest 30 minutes of my life, sitting with Jon's head on my leg. At first I couldn't think of anything to say, and then I asked him questions about all our adventures together, starting from when we were in first grade. Every now and then I caught a glimpse of Dad's worried, blood-flecked face in the rear view mirror. The spruce trees flew by as we broke every traffic law.

Finally we arrived in Healy. The EMT staff gave Jon plasma. "Lucky it's a nice day. The Life Flight from Fairbanks will be here soon."

The EMTs loaded Jon on a gurney and then onto the chopper when it arrived. Mr. Clellan climbed in too. Dad and I watched the flight take off. Dad put his arm on my shoulder. "We can only hope he lives. He may lose his foot."

It was a long day by the time we got back to the cabin, locked it up and loaded all the machines onto the trailer in the pitch black winter night with stars winking overhead.

Dad's cell phone rang when we were almost home. "He'll live, after five pints of blood."

I closed my eyes and leaned back on the headrest.

That weekend broke me of my addiction to gore. Now blood of any kind makes me queasy.

But I have a new fascination. Girls.

Monster

Halibut can grow to 8 feet long and weigh 700 pounds. The largest caught sport fishing was 459 pounds. Large halibut are usually females.

"You are so careless," I say to Tyler as I watch him fish his gear out of the water.

"The tide came up fast, Rob. The least you could do is help." Tyler trips over something under the surf and comes up sputtering. "It's not funny," he chokes, water streaming from his nose. "This water's freezing."

I stop laughing and walk across the beach to help him up. The sea water in Resurrection Bay is probably 50 degrees this time of year. Tyler's teeth are already chattering. "Did you get everything?"

He nods, looking like a drowned rat. We are packing our kayaks on the beach, ready to paddle four miles out to a cabin.

"I should send you with Mom and Dad along the hiking trail," I say. "You could still catch them."

"No." Tyler stamps his foot, which sends a geyser of water over the top of his boot. "Just because you're older doesn't mean you're the boss. And just because it's your birthday you can't get everything your way."

I had forgotten. "Sixteen. And smart, too," I say, tapping my skull.

He flattens me for that, and I guess I deserve it. He might be younger, but he's strong. Sand flies like a tornado until I finally get him pinned.

"Now we both have to change," Ty says, pushing me off and spitting sand from his mouth.

"Small price for winning." I flex my considerable bicep.

"You're a moron." Ty stomps off to change.

It's mighty quiet as we shove our gear into hatches in the bow and stern of the plastic sea kayaks and put on our life jackets and spray skirts.

"You look like a girl," Ty snickers.

"We're twin sissies, then."

Ty primps his hair.

"Pansy." I jam a piece of herring on my hook, rinse my hands in the water, and stow my pole under the bungees on the kayak as I push off from shore. I hear Ty mumbling as he gets in his boat. "You're my idol, Rob," I think he says. Confidently I cast my line and re-stow my rod.

"Are you sure that's a good idea? You might hook something big. Oh, that's right. It's *you* with the rod."

He's referring to my poor luck on the last few trips. "I've caught more in the day than you." Actually, Ty's a good fisherman. I taught him all I know.

Ty powers his kayak ahead.

I struggle along behind. What's wrong, anyway? We've only been paddling for 20 minutes, but my arms are tired and I still haven't caught up.

Finally Ty stops and waits for me. "What's wrong, big bro? Feeling weak today?" He grins.

"I'm fine," I huff, trying not to sound as winded as I am.

"Must not've checked your hatches after you changed."

I stop paddling, smelling a rat. "You didn't."

He nods. "Put at least 40 pounds of rock in your back hatch."

I give him credit for doing all that work without me noticing. "That's nothing." I need strength training for football this year anyway and I don't want to give him the satisfaction. I set off at a steady pace trying to ignore the weight dragging me back.

"Rob, your reel's stripped."

I ignore him and paddle on. He is such a trickster. "Honest."

I turn to look and can't believe my eyes. I must not have set the bail after I cast! There's probably 200 feet of line in the water! I grab the rod and start reeling, knocking my paddle into the water.

"Who's the klutz now?"

"Get the paddle, would ya?" I say, reeling away. Some time for a joke.

"Thank God nothing bit. You've got to be close to the bottom."

Suddenly my line goes taut and the force swings my bow around, practically pulling me in. Only someone with balance like a cat could've stayed in the boat.

"Rob! Hang on!"

"It's only the bottom, Ty."

"The bottom doesn't move, and that thing's moving!"

It doesn't take long to see I am being towed around by a huge bottom feeder, maybe a halibut, maybe a ray. For the next half hour all I can do is hang on for dear life and let the fish tire out. Each time she stops I reel in, but as soon as she feels resistance off she goes again.

Good old Tyler splashes along behind. He's had the presence of mind to bungee my wayward paddle to his deck. I can hear him better than I can see him. "Mom will kill you if you fall in."

"Kill me? I'll die first!" The line zips out again and all I can do is keep from being dragged in.

"How big do you think that halibut is?"

"The size of a small car."

"What're you gonna do with it?"

What I'm going to do with it is the last thing on my mind. Staying afloat is first.

"Don't look now, Rob. You've got an audience."

"What are you looking at?" I yell toward two motor boats nearby. "Haven't you ever caught a fish before?"

Suddenly the monster changes direction and bends my rod double under the kayak before spinning me around like a cork. As I whiz by one of the boats the cutest girl I've ever seen is watching.

"My brother's catching a halibut," I hear Ty say from behind.

I think I hear an exclamation of approval from the boat. Or maybe it is a loud laugh.

"Need a hand?" a guy from the other boat yells.

I'm about ready to ask for help.

"My brother can handle it, right Rob?"

My arms feel like they'll be ripped from their sockets at any minute. But then I see the girl again and get a burst of adrenaline. Or maybe the old fish is tiring after pulling around a kayak full of gear and rocks, but I am going to get a look at the fish or die. I pull up and reel down, over and over. Sweat pours down my face and lands on my spray skirt and I keep pulling.

"You're gaining on it, Rob!" Ty is rafted up next to me now and between the two of us we're too big an anchor for the fish to fight.

I know she is too big to land on a kayak as she roils to the surface, but nothing prepares me for the monstrous eyeballs I see, as big as two garbage can lids.

"Holy Halibut!" Ty exclaims as a flick of her whale-sized tail lifts us in the air at the same moment my line snaps.

Then everything is quiet.

I lay my head on my aching arms and try to catch my breath. "Did you get a picture, Ty?"

"You have the camera."

It figures. "No one will believe it." The biggest fish I almost caught is 200 feet down by now.

Ty hands me my paddle and re-hooks and re-baits my line, handing the rod over. "You'll get the next one."

I give it back. "Your turn, Ty. I'm outta gas."

"Really?" He looks like he's going to cry in his excitement.

"I don't want to have all the fun." I pick up my paddle and feebly aim toward Caine's Head.

I hear the whirr of the reel as he casts, then the click of the bail. Ty will troll for salmon as I had intended, a much safer way to fish from a kayak. "Mom'll love it if we come in with a fresh silver salmon."

I nod, wondering if my aching muscles will make it the two remaining miles before she sends out the Coast Guard to find her overdue sons.

Ty laughs. "You screamed like a girl when that halibut spun you like a cork."

I'm too tired to reply.

"That cute girl heard you scream. I think she smiled."

She'll never see me again, I hope.

Ty looks thoughtful. "She'll be talking about you to all her friends. Your love life could use a boost."

"Shut up and paddle."

Ty chuckles. "Thank God I put those rocks in your boat!"

A Whale of a Tail

A humpback whale has pectoral fins on both sides of the body, as do right and blue whales. In contrast, gray and minke whales have pectoral fins angled down. The leading edge of a humpback's pectoral fin is often covered with sharp barnacles.

"You've got to stay in Resurrection Bay," Dad says handing me the key to the boat.

"Yes, sir."

"We'll meet you back here at the dock at five sharp."

I nod. "Sure you and Mom don't want to come?"

Dad looks at Mom. "We have other plans."

They watch us climb aboard our 22' aluminum Lund. "Cast us off, Dad." They do nothing but stand with their arms crossed.

"Put your lifejacket on, Rob," Tyler whispers as he makes a show of tightening his.

Dad casts us off when I've got my jacket on.

"Rob, I'm counting on you to be back on time. Not like last week at Caine's Head."

"And no crazy stories about huge halibut with eyes the size of trash can lids," Mom adds.

"I've got it. Back in time, not strange stories, fish we can eat. Seriously, I'm not a kid any more." I wave as I engage the engine.

I putter the boat out of the harbor past the hundreds of slips housing other boats, most with motors bigger than ours.

"Rob!" Ty points to a boat nearby. "It's that girl you think is cute!"

I turn to follow his pointed finger. For the briefest moment our eyes meet and it's love at first sight. My stomach flips as she waves.

"I think she recognizes us from our halibut adventure."

"She's in love with me," I mumble.

"Close your mouth before you drool," Ty says slapping me on the shoulder. "I'm Ty," he yells to the sexy girl over the sound of the engine.

"I'm Jasmine."

"My brother thinks you're hot."

My hand, so in complete control one moment before, hits the throttle with that comment and the boat lurches forward throwing Ty to the deck and knocking my shades from my face before I get it back under control. Jasmine covers her mouth with her hand. Maybe she's worried about her true love, I think, but I can tell from her exotic brown eyes she's laughing.

"Great, Ty. Why'd you have to say that?" I still can't believe it. "That was so uncool."

"Why'd you have to knock me to the deck?"

I don't tell him it was an accident. "You deserved it."

"Don't pout. You look stupid in that lifejacket anyway."

I can't keep my mind off Jasmine as I rev the engine once we're outside the No Wake zone. Those big brown eyes, the shiny long hair tied back in a ribbon, her perfect figure.

Ty interrupts my reverie. "I'll rig the poles and we can troll for salmon."

I nod and I'm semi-conscious of Ty applying cut herring to the rigs, reeling out lengths of line, and setting two poles in the rod holders. It's overcast but not too cold and Ty cracks open a soda out on the back deck.

I'm entertaining Jasmine on a yacht in the Caribbean. She looks great in a bikini, and I look pretty good in my Speedo, at least what I can see of myself.

Jasmine approaches carrying two frozen drinks, the kind with the little umbrella sticking out. I can't believe my luck—Jasmine, a yacht, sunshine. She leans in to kiss me with those luscious lips...

"Rob, let's try another spot. We haven't even gotten a nibble. Why do you have a goofy grin on your face?"

"What grin?" I look around. I can see several boats in the area and no one's having a lot of luck.

"Maybe the fish aren't in yet."

Can't he tell I'm just not into fish today?

Ty comes up to me. He puts a hand on my forehead. "Fish, Rob. Fish."

Nothing. It's no use. I can't keep my mind off Jasmine.

Ty looks like he's putting two and two together. "I think that's Jasmine's boat over in the cluster of boats by Bear Glacier."

Really? I grab the binoculars. It does look like her boat. "I think they're having more luck over there." I turn the wheel. "Reel in. We'll zip over."

I wait until Ty has secured the poles and open up the engine.

Once across the Bay, I weave my way expertly through the group of boats, keeping an eye out for Jasmine's, an unusual turquoise color.

"The fishing looks a little slow, Rob."

Sure enough, no one seems to be catching anything. I spot the boat. It's anchored and it looks like Jasmine's family has opted to try their luck bottom fishing.

"Maybe we could try for some halibut or rock fish," Ty suggests.

"Great idea." I steer closer, but not rudely close to Jasmine's boat.

"Hey, there's…"

"Not another word from you, Ty. And get the halibut rods geared up. I'll drop anchor."

"This'll be good, Rob. Now we can both fish."

I nod. "I get this side. The view's nice."

Ty winks at me.

I drop my halibut hook, herring, and three pound weight into the water and let out the bail. Two hundred feet of line disappears into the green water before I hit bottom and lock the bail.

Jasmine looks up and waves. The rocking of the boat moves the bait to lure the fish, but I work the rod like the pro I am. I tip my hat back and unzip my jacket so she can see my chiseled features.

Ty's rod tip is pulled toward the water. "I've got one, Rob!"

"Steady Tyler. And keep your tip up," I advise loudly as I reel in.

"I know how to catch a fish." He sees me point a discreet thumb at the other boat. "Help, Big Brother. I need a lot of muscle to land this brute," he mocks.

The fish makes a run for it and strips line off the reel. Maybe it actually is a big one.

Ty heaves and reels and it comes to the surface, probably a 30-pounder. "We'll keep it," Ty says immediately. I gaff it and haul it aboard, then make a show about stunning it with a club so it stops thrashing against the hull.

"Thanks, O Mighty Brother."

I feel proud. So far I haven't seen their boat land a fish.

"You've got a trail of fish blood across your face."

I opt to leave it. I'm sure I look rakish and manly.

Within minutes Ty's hooked into another fish. This one comes in with less fight but it's slightly larger.

"I'll keep it."

"It'll be your limit."

"I'm keeping it anyway. I'll spend the rest of my time watching My Fishing Hero pull in a big one in front of his girl."

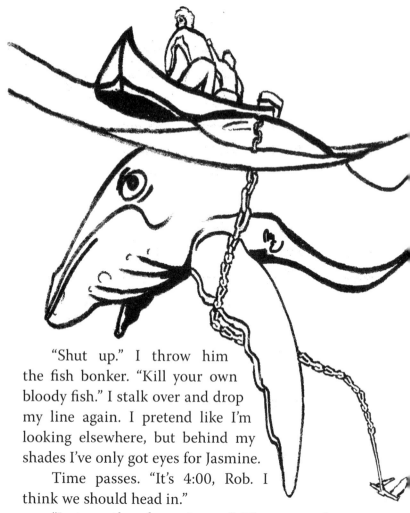

"Shut up." I throw him the fish bonker. "Kill your own bloody fish." I stalk over and drop my line again. I pretend like I'm looking elsewhere, but behind my shades I've only got eyes for Jasmine.

Time passes. "It's 4:00, Rob. I think we should head in."

"Just another few minutes." The scenery's too good to leave right now.

Jasmine points toward our boat and aims binoculars right at us. I tip my hat and smile. She points again and others on her boat gather and begin waving at me. I wave back. Someone aims a camera at me, the kind with the huge lens. I must be looking good. I put on my best smile.

"Rob!" Ty yells. I turn in time to see a geyser of water erupt from the blowhole of a whale not 25 feet from the boat, and the arch of a back as long as a school bus, then the flip of a gigantic tail as the whale dives. Our boat rises on an upwelling of water.

"Wow. That was unbelievable."

Then the boat lurches forward so powerfully Ty is on his butt again in the fish slime and I drop the rod, trying to get my hands on the boat.

"What's happening?"

The boat is being pulled forward faster than it has a right to go without the engine on. We zip by Jasmine's boat and I get a glimpse of concerned faces turned our way. "Somehow we're attached to the whale by our anchor line. It's the only explanation."

Ty looks scared. "What're we gonna do?"

"I'll get the manual on whale emergencies and check." I'm hanging on to the side of the boat for dear life.

"It's not funny."

It's not funny, unless we survive. Then maybe we'll have a laugh over it. "Make sure your life jacket's tight. I'll get our survival gear."

By the time I'm back on the deck with two bright orange suits, the whale is closer to the surface to breathe and I can see the anchor line on its pectoral fin. The whale is towing us with good speed toward the mouth of the Resurrection Bay.

"Mom and Dad said don't leave the Bay."

"Tell that to the whale. I don't think they imagined this when they cast us off." Jasmine's boat is trailing us. The whale dives and pulls our boat forward in a rush.

"We're gonna die!" Ty yells, and this time I think he might be right. By some miracle we stay afloat.

When the whale surfaces and breathes, he rolls over on one side, then the other, as if to shake us.

"Just stop swimming!" Ty yells.

Suddenly I get an idea, grab the key and start the engine. When the whale dives again I race the engine and give it full throttle, right over the area the whale vacated.

"Are you crazy?" Ty has his arms over his head. "I can't watch."

Suddenly the boat stops. I hold my breath and Ty uncovers his head. A whale breaches ahead of us, rising up out of the water, twisting, and splashing down again.

"It's free."

Ty comes over and gives me an unfeigned hug of relief. "You saved our lives!"

"Only to have Dad kill us when we get back late." It's past meeting time and we are at least half an hour from the dock.

Jasmine's boat pulls up next to ours. She has a look of concern on her face. Probably thought she'd never see me again.

"Are you boys okay?" a man asks. "Never seen anything like that before. Reminds me of that kayak being towed by the halibut last weekend. Some people are nuts."

Ty and I look at each other and he starts to smirk.

"Thanks for asking. We're fine," I say before Ty breaks into all out laughter.

"That was some nifty driving."

I shrug, like this kind of thing happens every day. "It was nothing, really."

"We've got to get back, Rob."

I pull the boat away. "Rob," I hear Jasmine say, as if it's the sweetest name in the world. "Call me," she mouths.

I almost turn back. One more look at her would be worth any amount of anger from Dad. "Did you hear that? She wants me to call her."

"Did you get her number?"

I try to turn the boat around, but Ty wrestles the wheel from me and aims toward the dock.

Half an hour later we're pulling into the boat harbor. Mom and Dad are waiting and neither look too pleased.

Ty goes to the back deck and hauls up a halibut with a huge smile on his face. "Dinner!"

"Looks like a nice fish, boys."

"They're both mine."

Dad looks at me, empty-handed again.

"Honest, Dad. You should've…"

He rolls his eyes. "…seen the one that got away. I've heard that before."

For the Love of Dogs

The Alaskan Husky sled dog is a mixed breed selected to pull large loads for long distances. An Alaskan Husky is usually less than 50 pounds in weight. An individual dog can pull a load up to 800 pounds. Getting dogs to pull together requires hours of practice.

Twelve excited dogs in harness, Jack stood on the runners of his sled and practically flew through the snowy landscape. The dogs, barking and crazy with anticipation in the yard moments before were all business now, running straight and true on a path they knew well, between tall evergreens.

"In a week we'll be on a new path in the Junior Iditarod," Jack said to the dogs. He had a habit of talking to them when they were together, which was as often as Jack could manage between his homework and house chores.

Nothing beat the freedom of being out on the trail with his dogs. It made the long hours and intensive labor of caring for them around the yard, harnesses made and mended, all worthwhile.

The sled powered by twelve dogs made good time. It was almost as if they had wings. Jack's eyes watered even now in the frigid air and he snapped on his goggles. It wouldn't do to freeze his corneas this close to the race. The dogs needed him to be at his best if they had a chance to win, and Jack believed they had a good chance.

He jumped off his sled and ran beside the team as the dogs began a long uphill section. He carried a load in his sled similar to the one he'd have in the race and he wanted his dogs fresh. Besides, he needed to be in shape too, and that meant training. "Straight on, Gibson and Paul Reed." His dogs were all raised from the family kennel, and most were named after guitar brands. Guitars were Jack's other passion.

At the top of the hill, Taylor, his only female but one of his lead dogs, tried to go left onto their usual trail. "Gee, Taylor and Martin," he called to his lead dogs. Jack wanted to have a longer run today on a path less familiar to the dogs. After some initial confusion in the leads, the dogs straightened themselves out and began pulling well.

It was then that a moose charged into the middle of the team. Gibson and PR were down under the weight of the thrashing moose which became entangled in the line. That only caused him to buck and kick even more. Martin swung the dogs back around aggressively against the moose.

"Stop, Martin, Taylor!" Moose attacks were deadly on a team and Jack couldn't afford to have the entire group within range of the sharp hooves. Jack jumped off the sled and ran to the fray. It was a mess of lines as

dogs jumped over each other to escape or nip at the moose. Two of the dogs, Fender and Peavey, were fighting each other in the confusion. Alvarez and Dean looked as if they were being choked by their harnesses and the pulling of the other dogs.

"My gun." Jack hadn't grabbed his gun, buried in the basket of the sled, but when PR went under the feet of the moose and blood blossomed crimson onto the white snow Jack laid into the moose with his nearest weapon, a ski pole. The moose retreated into the woods, surprised by the attack. Perhaps it thought the dogs were a pack of wolves, perhaps it had met its match.

"Stay away!" Jack yelled at the moose, and then surveyed his dogs. Some were still pulling toward the moose. PR was down in a bloody, churned up mess of snow.

Jack ignored the others and knelt by one of his strongest dogs. PR lifted his head weakly as Jack palpated his legs for fractures. A gaping wound along his back, still bleeding freely, revealed muscle and fascia. PR needed help right away.

The moose attacked again while Jack knelt by his dogs. This time he had to dive and roll free to avoid becoming a victim himself as the whole frenzy of dogs jumping and pulling and the moose lunging and kicking started all over.

An angry moose could destroy an entire team, and this one seemed to have it in for them. Jack ran to the sled, pulled out his .44 Magnum and unloaded a few rounds into the moose, which stumbled away from the team before going to his knees, Taylor and Martin on his heels.

"Taylor, Martin, back!" Jack lunged for their lines to pull them away as he shot once more to bring the moose down. He put the safety on the gun and dropped it in the basket, amazingly still upright on the runners. He grabbed a burlap bag and ran toward PR. First he applied pressure to stop the bleeding, then unclipped PR's harness from the gang line, wrapping him in the bag. He carried the dog to the basket of the sled and nestled him into his sleeping bag. "Hang in there, buddy, while we get everyone untangled."

He surveyed the rest of the team. Gibson was standing on three legs and bled from a smaller wound than his harness mate. Jack dressed the wound and ran his hand down the right foreleg. "Broken for sure, but you'll live." Gibson looked downtrodden as Jack took him off the line and placed him in the basket by his brother.

The rest of the dogs were standing on all fours, anyway, though the lines were in complete disarray. "I don't have time for this," Jack said, thinking of the injured dogs.

He set to the mess as quickly as he could, unclipping dogs and staking them to the side, untwisting and unknotting leads. Sweating in the freezing air, he finally turned the sled around on the narrow path and laid out his main line. Now he ran each of the dogs to their spots. Fender, he decided belatedly, tail down and head dragging, was also hurt and ended up in the already crowded basket. Jack discarded gear to make room for all three dogs.

PR was still breathing but didn't open his eyes when Fender was put next to him. "I can't lose you, PR," Jack said, running his hand across the soft black head.

Jack jumped onto the runners and let up the brake. "Home!" As the dogs took off he turned to watch the limp figure of the moose that created so much havoc fade into the distance. He hated him for wrecking his team, but knew he acted on natural instinct. His

Dad and brother Will would return in the morning to butcher the moose, if wolves didn't get him first.

It seemed to take forever to cover the few miles to home. In the yard, deafened with the noise of dogs greeting each other, Jack applied the brake and ran into the house. "Moose attack," he said to his dad.

In minutes they had the three injured dogs inside the house, while Will unhitched the others. "Get some IV fluids for PR," his dad said.

Jack helped his dad, an expert in dog care, put a line into an unresisting PR. There were no veterinarians in the area, so local mushers had to do all their own work. They injected an anesthetic and sewed PR up with sutures. "He's lost a lot of blood, but he's tough. I give him a 50/50 chance. Keep him warm and comfortable."

Jack's Dad shone a flashlight into Fender's eyes. "Concussion, I think. We'll keep him inside tonight too and watch for seizures. He'll be fine by morning."

Jack felt a weight lift from his shoulders. Maybe he wouldn't lose any of the dogs.

"You stitch up Gibson while I get the plaster for his leg."

Gibson wouldn't hold still until they injected him with a sedative. Then Jack stitched first muscle, then skin as best he could. His dad nodded in approval at the neat black row of stitches. They set and applied a cast to the broken leg.

Jack grabbed a blanket and pillow and sat against the wall, surrounded by his injured dogs, determined to stay awake all night. The moose attack played through his mind as if on a film reel. He should have gone for the gun right away. He shouldn't have taken a new trail in the dark. He should have had Will along for safety. Could he have prevented the whole awful incident? On and on his thoughts raced.

Each dog's face appeared in his mind as he mulled over their position in the team. Martin was probably too aggressive to be lead dog. Jack feared Martin may have made the moose angrier by swinging the team around. Maybe he should bring along another female, like Epiphone, who had been left behind tonight. He relived the moments PR, Gibson, and Fender were injured. Gibson. PR. Fender...

Gibson's whining woke him early in the dark Alaskan morning. "Bathroom, boy?"

Fender joined him at the door and he led the two dogs into the yard, then back inside. Jack plopped down next to PR and stroked his head. "You're the best dog," he whispered. PR was deathly still. His dogs were so important to him; Jack knew he'd cry like a baby if one died. Living in Bush Alaska they were just about his only friends. He could rely on the dogs to always be there for him, to give him their best, and to enjoy his company. Most he had raised from pups. Losing even one dog would be heartbreaking.

While he thought about PR he ran his hands along the black back, the ridged ribs, and the four white legs to the paws. He massaged PR's feet. "You used to be so tiny—now you're the biggest." Then back to the head and the soft ears, back, belly and legs again. Over and over, while Gibson and Fender slept against him.

Jack woke in the gray morning light, a soft tongue licking his face. Gibson and Fender were gone. PR's eyes were open and his head up. Jack draped an arm over PR's neck. "You're gonna make it."

Hanging in There

Glacier travel over snow is dangerous. For safety, one part-
ner usually "pickets", or sets an anchor into the snow or ice, as he
belays the other partner forward for about 50 feet of the climbing
rope connecting them. The forward partner then applies a picket
and the back partner moves ahead. The two "leap frog" across
the glacier.

One second he is there, the next second he's
gone and the 50 foot section of climbing rope
connecting us tightens and pulls me to my knees. I'm
dragged forward in a rush, clutching my picket and
praying it holds. I take my first breath once the rope
has quit dragging me toward the snow-covered crevasse that has opened beneath my climbing partner
Dave's feet.

My second breath is a frantic one. "Dave!"

Silence.

"Dave!"

Nothing but me in an expanse of white emptiness,
our purple and blue rope, a lifeline for Dave, trailing to
nothing.

I have a moment to ponder utter loneliness and the fear of being on this mountain by myself before I realize only quick action will save us. Still lying on the snow and grasping my picket, I beat in an ice screw for good measure, looping my rope through. I get to my knees and wonder if the practice on the glacier closer to home has prepared us for the real thing. And this is it.

I climb to my feet. "Dave!"

Nothing. I measure with my eyes the amount of rope lying on the snow. Twenty five feet or so, I guess. That leaves about 25 more dangling into the crevasse with Dave on the end.

I probe with my ax as I approach the crevasse. It's death if we both fall in. The crunch of my crampons and boots is deafening as my ears strain for a sound from Dave.

At the end of the rope I see what happened. A snow bridge over the crevasse has given way under Dave's feet. Because he was in lead, he took the fall.

I finally hear Dave's voice. "Matt? Matt! Where are you?"

"I'm here buddy!" I peer into the yawning blue and white mouth of the glacier holding Dave but can't see him. It must undercut and he's directly beneath me.

"Matt." I hear a whimper, almost a sob. "It took you so long to get here."

It must have seemed an eternity to Dave, I realize, hanging there like a ragdoll over nothingness and death, wedged into the glacier. I shiver imagining it. "Are you hurt?"

"My shoulder's killing me. I think it's dislocated."

When the snow gives way, most people tumble head first into the crevasse, often hitting their head or limbs on sharp edges of ice. Then the rope and harness provide a huge jolt arresting the fall. All in all, it's not easy on the body. "Did you black out?"

"I think so."

He couldn't have been unconscious long. I cross my fingers, hoping he doesn't have a brain injury and thankful we agreed to wear helmets. "What day is it?"

"Tuesday. I'm okay, Matt, except for my arm. May have broken my nose, too."

"I can't see you, Dave. Are you close to the wall?" A crevasse is an uneven piece of work. I hope Dave can anchor himself to the wall and maybe even help climb out.

I hear muffled curses. "My ice axe is on the right side of my pack. Can't reach it with my useless arm."

"I'm going to get you out," I say with more confidence than I feel. He sounds close to panic.

"I'm scared, Matt, and it's freezing down here. You can't believe how cold it is. My pack's dragging me down."

The trip had started so well. Dave and I were flown onto this glacier in the Wrangell Mountains under a crisp spring blue sky. We spent five days exploring the ice field and summiting a 10,000 foot nameless peak. That night as we cooked dinner in our tent we labeled our map. "Dave and Matt's Peak" it now says forever.

I run through rescue scenarios in my mind. Dave's not going to be able to help. I'll have to pull him out myself, and in that case, it'll have to be a Z-pulley. I've only practiced this kind of rescue once, just before the trip.

"Matt, my arm's killing me."

I examine my climbing gear. In a stroke of luck, the Z-pulley kit is still rigged from our practice session.

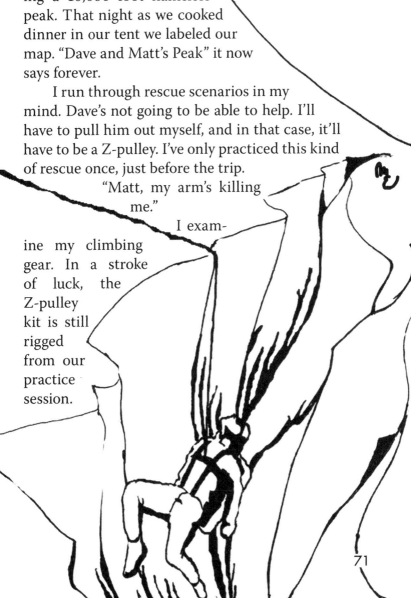

"Dave, I need you to hang in there and help me out. Are you with me?"

"The pack's gotta come off, Matt."

"We can't lose your pack!" Getting Dave out before he becomes hypothermic will be touch and go. We'll need his gear to survive the night. "I'm setting a Z-pulley. When it's ready I'll come back and let you know."

I scramble to set several more ice screws in a Z formation from the edge of the crevasse and backward. I'm at the end and the Z should give me a mechanical advantage to hoist Dave out. I wiggle a tool under the rope trailing over the edge of the crevasse. Ice crystals can fray a climbing rope under the load of Dave's weight and my pulley action.

"Dave, I'm anchored in and I'm going to get you out. It could take some time and I can't hear you unless I'm at the opening."

"I can't hear you either." There's a pause. "Don't leave me, Matt."

"We're getting you out, like I said."

"How long?" Dave's voice is thick with worry.

I don't know exactly how much rope separates Dave from the top of the crevasse, but I know it is slow, back-breaking work to haul someone out. It may take two hours. I shiver. I hope Dave can last that long. "I'll work as quickly as I can."

"Don't drop me. My arm can't take any more trashing."

Hand over hand, inch by inch, I pull on that rope. My arms ache, my back feels tight, and I'm sweating under all my layers. Still, I keep going as the white, barren landscape dims around me. The coming of evening is yet another danger. I try to gauge my progress by measuring with my eyes the loops of rope I've already pulled through. I have no idea if Dave's still alive or if all I'm doing is breaking my back hauling a corpse. I long for the company and help of another person. No one materializes on the featureless horizon. I keep going. Finally, I see Dave's gloved hand grasp the edge of the snow. "Don't try to help. It'll be slow going no matter what." My mouth is dry, my voice creaky and uneven.

Finally Dave is on the edge of the crevasse. I go to him and help him to his feet. He can hardly stand. His face is pinched with pain, his gloveless, dangling hand purple and white. He puts his good arm around me, half hug, half support.

When I see Dave my relief turns to fear. He looks horrible. There's a gash across one cheek and his nose is purple and swollen. "Get your glove on or you'll lose your hand." It already looks like he has frostbite.

"Lost the glove when I fell. It was colder than a deep freeze down there."

I rummage through my pack for an extra set of gloves. Exposure is death to skin at these temperatures.

I hand him some gloves and he grimaces as we put the dangling hand in. "I can't carry a pack."

I scan ahead. We need to make camp as soon as possible, eat food and warm up. Dave's at the end of his energy and is starting to shake. Somehow he's standing but I can tell he won't be for long.

"We're walking to that hump of snow and rock over there. It'll act as a wind block. I'll drag your pack but I need you to walk." I feel fatigue creeping into my bones and push it away.

Dave nods. We'll never make it if we set pickets. We'll take our chances and walk together. If we happen on another crevasse, we'll go down together. I quickly take up the screws and instead rig a set of ropes to his pack so I can drag it. We walk a quarter of a mile to the camp spot. By that time Dave's good arm is over my shoulder and he's really dragging. His breath comes in gasps.

"I can't catch my breath."

I know we don't have much time. Dave looks like he's in shock. I throw my pack to the ground and drag his next to me as well. "Get the stove out of my pack."

I grab the tent and set it up as quickly as I can, not even looking to see if he's done his job. I lay out both foam pads and sleeping bags.

Dave is sitting on the snow, leaned up against his pack, semiconscious with the stove gripped in his hand. I slap him in the face. "Get up. We've got to get you in the bag."

I wrestle him into the bag, clothes and all. I grab the stove and fuel it up, right in the tent. We need warmth. I start to shiver as my sweat-soaked under layer cools. I throw soup mix and all our extra sugar into the boiling water then strip down and put dry clothes on in the very cramped space. I can tell the tent is heating up as I pour a mug of the strange soup for each of us. I prop Dave up. He's shivering but not shaking anymore.

"Drink this." I help him down the steamy liquid.

"What is it? It's disgusting."

"Keep drinking."

We finish that and start on seconds. Neither one of us is shivering by the time we're eating energy bars.

"You saved my life."

"Don't get sappy on me," I say, but inside I feel choked up. What would I do without Dave?

"Let's take a look at you." I reach inside the bag and press on his collar bone and ribs. The shoulder is obviously dislocated. This injury is common in climbing and I think I can help. "I'm going to relocate your shoulder."

Dave pales. I pre-position his arm to the side and place my other hand on the front of his shoulder, pushing down. It's almost an audible sound as the shoulder repositions.

"Trying to knock me out again?" Dave says through gritted teeth. "I think I'm going to puke."

I quit my prodding. "Don't. We just spent an hour filling you up with food." I cinch his arm to his body with an extra strap to protect it. "You're going to need a doctor as soon as possible."

"We're in the middle of nowhere, Matt."

I shrug like it's no big deal. We have a rendezvous point to reach by tomorrow and we'll never make it with Dave in this shape. I look at the frostbitten hand. It doesn't look much better. I don't tell Dave he may lose his fingers.

As he dozes, I look at the GPS and the map. I figure we're at least ten miles from where we need to be.

We could get up early and try to walk out, but we'd be leaving Dave's pack behind. The risk is unacceptable. We'll have to stay put and hope for a clear sky and a pilot able to spot us and land close by.

"They may have to send a chopper in for us."

I close the map. "Didn't know you were awake."

"I can't make it out on my own. We gotta stay with our shelter."

I nod and get dinner prepared, anxious now about whether we have enough food. On the one hand, Dave needs to eat. On the other, we may be stuck on this ice cube longer than expected. That solves it. He'll eat and I'll pass even though my stomach growls with hunger. "We'll save some food for tomorrow."

Dave nods. It's well past dark and extremely quiet as he finishes dinner. I sip instant coffee. The day has caught up to me and I can barely keep my eyes open, but I have to stay awake and watch Dave. Pulmonary edema, brain hematoma, concussion; the list of possible injuries scares me awake. I'll have to wake him periodically during the night.

"Get in your bag or you'll fall over where you are."

"I'm not tired. You sleep." It's very quiet in the middle of nowhere.

"Quiet's good. No wind for our rescue."

I nod. He's right. "Let's hope for the best. We've gotta get you out of here."

"I've always wanted a chopper rescue," Dave mutters before falling asleep.

In grey morning light we fix coffee and eat energy bars, dress and exit the tent.

"Clear and calm. Perfect for a rescue."

I stomp my feet. "Frigid. Back to the bags." Before I return to the tent I lay out our 150 feet of rope spelling "SOS". I roll a piece of my foam sleeping pad and douse it with fuel.

At our scheduled pick up time I light the foam roll and the resulting thick, black smoke billows into the blue sky. I scan the horizons, hoping our pilot spots the smoke and then us. We don't talk, Dave and I, each contemplating the situation and all the potential outcomes.

Just as we're about ready to give up hope and get back into the tent, we hear a plane engine and wave our arms. The plane circles once, tipping a wing.

"He saw us for sure," Dave says, a real smile on his face.

"I think so. Nothing to do now but wait."

"Wait and eat. I'm starving."

"Think we should save some food for tomorrow?"

"They'll get us today, I bet."

Dave eats, I nibble. As the sun sets we realize it'll be another night on the ice.

"I'm feeling almost good enough to pack out," Dave says.

"We're staying put. They know where we are and they'll come to get us."

"Sorry, Matt. It's not what we planned."

"It's okay. You gotta take what life deals."

That night the wind picks up and it starts to snow. By morning there is a foot of fresh stuff blanketing the world. I'm beginning to feel claustrophobic with time spent in the tent.

"They'll never be able to land and we're almost out of food," Dave says.

"The wind has died down. Nothing to do but wait. They'll be here." I say it with more confidence than I feel.

We play poker until we hear the unmistakable sound of a chopper.

"They've sent a Pavehawk for us!" Dave can't disguise the excitement in his voice.

We leave all our gear in the tent. They won't wait for us to pack, and they won't take gear.

"All our climbing stuff," Dave says.

It's a loss I'm trying not to think about. I grab the map and a few small items and shove them in my pockets. "You go first." I steady the basket while he climbs in.

As the basket comes down again I climb aboard. It's a rush as I'm hoisted up and into the copter.

Dave and I get belted in by a soldier and we're whisked off the mountain toward home.

"You never know how an adventure will end," Dave says over the engine noise.

"You never do."

Bear Attack

Bear attacks on humans are relatively uncommon in Alaska. When a bear does attack, it is usually to protect a cub or a source of food, like a recent moose kill.

"Eight miles to go by the map," Tim says.

"My GPS says 8.5," I reply.

"Close enough. About three hours at the rate we travel."

Our group of five friends is finishing a trip along the Resurrection Trail. "I'll be glad to hit the car." It's a cool morning, and foggy. I feel the dampness in my clothing as it clings to me more than usual.

"Gotta get this pack off a minute," Caleb says. "I'm starving."

Tim grimaces. "You're always starving. Why don't you keep food in your pocket?"

"Don't wanna be bear bait."

We laugh. "We haven't even seen scat, brother," Jeff says. He's a couple years older than us and has appointed himself the leader. I didn't want him to come but I know Mom felt better knowing he was along. Plus, he drives and I only have a permit.

Todd shivers, and a wisp of cloud obscures the trail ahead. I shiver too as my sweat has chilled with this small break.

"Todd and Bryan are cold." Jeff never misses anything. "Let's get back on the trail. We'll never get to the van at this rate."

Jeff gestures to me. I'm the pace setter, even though I'm the smallest. "Lead us home, Bryan."

The trail is large and well worn and there's no way to get lost even though visibility is poor. The group gets strung out a little as we always do.

"Look here," I say to Todd, the only guy in sight. "A moose calf haunch right in the middle of the trail." It's a cinnamon color, with a perfect tiny hoof.

"Moose calves are easy prey for bear."

We look around. There's nothing to see in the foggy landscape. "Don't see or hear anything."

Todd pinches his nose shut. "Sure stinks, though."

"Maybe it's the dead moose calf."

Todd shakes his head. "It looks fresh. There's not a fly on it."

By now the rest of the guys have caught up.

Jeff stoops to examine the haunch. "We need to stay closer together. Get the bear spray in your hands, just in case. And we're going to make a lot of noise."

Caleb's munching on another snack, Tim and Todd are getting the bear spray, and I've got to take a leak.

"We shouldn't stop for long. Leave your packs on," Jeff says.

I take a few steps away from the group and something hits me like a ton of bricks. I'm on the ground and shaken like I'm a toy, then dragged off the trail. I flip onto my stomach but pain shoots up my leg. I try to crawl onto the trail but something's got me by the head. I smell decay and death and hear screaming.

* * * * *

Everything is black, but I hear voices and water running nearby.

"He's moving."

I feel like I'm stuck in mud. Every movement is hard, and my head is wracked with pain. "Bryan, it's Todd. Tim's here too. You've been mauled by a bear. Stay still or you may start bleeding again."

"Odd?" I say. I can't talk. My face feels swollen and my tongue uncoordinated. "Gotta see."

"What'd he say?" Tim's voice.

"Say it slow." Todd. His voice is deeper.

"Ah wanna see."

Silence.

"Ah wanna see." I'm starting to get scared. What's wrong with me, anyway?

"Tell him." Todd.

"Jeff said not to."

"Ell me! Ell me! Ell me!" I pound the ground with each word. At least my arm works.

"Stop moving and stay calm, buddy. To hell with Jeff." Todd calms his voice. "Bryan, the bear got you pretty good. There are wounds on your face and head and one eye looks bad. We've got you bandaged, so that's why you can't see. Your leg's tore up, too. We carried you to the river and washed you up best we could."

"Used up the first aid kit." Tim.

I'm trying to take it all in. How badly am I hurt? I wish I could see.

"Sit," I demand.

"I'm helping him, Tim. I don't care what Jeff said and he's not here."

"As long as he doesn't start bleeding again I don't figure it'll be too bad."

Someone helps me sit up, making my head spin and pound. There's a metallic taste and my mouth's dry. "Drink."

Someone hands me a water bottle. My arms move and I drink, choking on the first mouthful.

"Little bits. Your throat's probably swollen." Todd.

Suddenly I'm glad I can't see myself. I drink mouthfuls. The water's delicious I'm so thirsty.

"Jeff and Caleb have gone for help." Tim.

"Stand."

"Bryan, why don't you lie down? We've got this sleeping bag here." Todd.

"Stand." I try to get up, pain jolting through my leg. I feel wooden boards rather than ground. A bridge.

"I say we let him do what he wants." Todd.

"Maybe he's delirious." Tim.

"Not. Help." I feel for the uprights so I can pull myself up. One of my legs is not cooperating.

"Easy, buddy." Todd.

I feel gentle hands on each side helping me rise. I grasp the railing of the bridge and my head spins.

"Water," I croak. There's another bottle in my hand and I remember to take it slow.

"Gatorade this time." Todd.

I down the whole container, leaning on the bridge. Tim and Todd have moved away and are discussing something I can't hear over the sound of moving water.

"Walk." My leg throbs but I want to get out of here.

"You can't walk, Bryan. Your leg, man, it's…"

"Walk." I drop the water bottle and hear it roll along the bridge.

"He's not bleeding and it could take a long time for help to come. And that bear could come back." Todd.

"Walk." I start walking. I have no idea where I'm going, but I feel my way along the bridge. "Walk. Walk. Walk," I say with each step. I'm cold and I want to move.

"Get another layer. He's shivering." Todd. "Listen, buddy, you can walk as long as you don't start bleeding. Let me help, though."

I nod. Sounds good to me. Someone's putting a soft jacket on my arm and I pull it on the rest of the way. Then my raincoat.

Tim and Todd are talking again. I wish I could hear what they're saying.

"Bryan, here's the plan. Tim's stashing our packs. He's gonna carry sleeping bags and food in his. We're going to head out."

"Good." Finally someone's talking sense.

My leg throbs as I wait for them. Boom. Boom. Boom. With each beat of my heart. I'm calm, but a little disoriented. I have no idea where I am, or what direction to go. I'm at the mercy of Todd and Tim.

"We've got to splint your leg or it may start bleeding." Todd. "You won't be able to bend your knee."

I can't bend it anyway. I nod. Anything to keep moving.

I feel something along my leg and the sound of duct tape being pulled off a roll. "We're bracing your leg with two hiking poles." Tim.

"Okay, Bryan, we're ready. I can't believe you're going to do this." Todd.

"Jeff will kill us." Tim.

I shrug and try to smile. Tim and Todd laugh. "You're the boss." Todd. "Take my arm."

I grab his arm at the elbow on my good side and use a pole in the other arm. I can hear Tim behind us and know he's got one, maybe two, canisters of bear spray back there. I don't know why. If she didn't kill me the first time, she probably won't be back again.

Todd and I learn to walk in step with each other. He tells me about obstacles in the trail. It's slow progress but my leg feels better when I'm moving.

I don't know how much time has passed when I trip over a root and Todd catches me. It jars my leg and I bend over in pain.

"Let's stop here, Bryan." Tim. He sounds worried.

"Walk." I've got to keep going.

"Have something to drink first. You've lost a lot of blood." Todd.

Again I down a whole bottle and haven't peed since the bear attack.

I take Todd's arm again, but my leg feels really stiff and I grimace.

"We should…"

"Walk."

"Put your arm over my shoulder." Todd. I feel his arm around my waist. "Left foot first."

I feel more secure and we continue in this way. At a steep section I drape my arm over Tim too and they carry me down.

I hear voices and the scratchy sound of a radio.

"It's Jeff, Caleb, and some EMTs with a rescue stretcher." I can hear the relief in Tim's voice.

But I want to keep going.

"What do you guys think you're doing?" Jeff.

"Ahm walking out."

"What'd he say?"

"He wants to walk, Jeff. We couldn't keep him down." Todd.

"I'm Mark and this is Rick. We're EMTs and we'd like to help." New voices.

I nod. They take my pulse and my blood pressure. They examine but don't remove my bandages or my leg splint. "Bryan, please turn your head slowly left and right." My head turns but my neck is sore.

"Bryan, we want to strap you to this board and carry you out."

The idea of lying down and being jostled all the way down the trail makes my head spin and I feel nauseous.

"Ahm walking out." I point to my head. "Izzy."

"I think his head hurts and he feels dizzy when he bends over or lies down." Todd.

There's a long discussion. I'm not included. I don't know why they don't ask me. I'm the one that's hurt. I start walking down the trail, blind. I feel someone grasp my elbow.

"Mark again. Bryan, we'll let you walk out with our help. If at any time you need the stretcher, or look like you're in trouble, we'll carry you out."

I nod.

"Tim and Jeff are going back to get the packs." I'm glad Todd's staying. He seems to understand me best. I grab his elbow, imagining the parade of people on the trail. Every now and then the radio goes off and one of the guys talks about our progress. Eventually I hear cars, and know the parking lot's nearby.

"Bryan, buddy, I can't believe you made it." Todd.

I nod. "All the way."

So that's how it happened. We made it back to the parking lot and Mark and Rick loaded me into the ambulance. I got a ride to Anchorage, but I walked the whole trail. All 35 miles of it.

They put my leg together with hundreds of stitches in the torn muscle and skin. It healed nicely, and now the only thing anyone notices is fading scars along my entire leg. I had surgery on my face, to fix my broken cheekbone and eye socket. They couldn't save my right eye, so now I have a glass one. It's a good party stopper when I pull it out. People tend to freak. Otherwise, no one even knows.

I still go hiking whenever I can, and I'm still the pacesetter. So, you see, even though I'm a little different, life's pretty much the same. People ask me if I'm worried about bears. I say no. What's the chance of being attacked twice?

Up a Creek without a Paddle

Beaver are plentiful in Alaska and even live in Anchorage, a modern city of about 300,000 people. Beaver can weigh up to 60 pounds. The dentin in their large incisor teeth turns red when they chew on spruce bark.

"Where'd you get that?" Tyler is lugging a deflated rubber kayak and a paddle up the driveway.

"Thought we could do Campbell Creek."

Campbell Creek runs through the heart of Anchorage and into Cook Inlet. We fish for salmon in the creek in fall. In summer it's a nice float, or so I've heard.

"There's only one paddle."

"We've got an old wooden one."

I'd forgotten about the wooden paddle. The last thing I remember doing with it is hitting rocks down the street.

"I'll go if you convince Mom." She'll have to drop us off and pick us up.

Ty shrugs. "She'll be glad to get us out of her hair."

Mom and Ty come out of the house moments later. Ty carries the old paddle, which is worse than I remember. It looks like Swiss cheese. Mom carries two life vests.

I can't believe she wants us to wear life vests. "Is Campbell Creek deep enough to drown in?"

"You'll wear these or you won't go." I take them from her and put one on right there in the driveway.

She rolls her eyes. "Good. Now you won't drown between here and the river." She opens the pocket on the vest and puts in a cell phone. "Call when you're done."

She drops us off behind the McDonald's on Tudor Road and hangs out while Ty and I take turns pumping up the kayak. "It looks like it's holding air." She seems dubious but satisfied. "Wear the life vests and be careful."

I put the pump in the car. "We're in Anchorage, Mom. Most of the creek is within sight of houses. What could go wrong?"

"With you boys, one never knows." Mom rolls up her window.

After this summer, I can't even think up a clever come back. "I'm sure it won't take long. It's only a few miles. Ty and I are good boaters."

Mom looks doubtful and mimes cell phone use as she drives away.

We carry the boat to the water's edge and Ty grabs the kayak paddle, with a blade on each end. "I'm driving so I get the seat in the back and the good paddle."

"I'm older. I get to navigate."

"I got the boat."

"You don't know what you're doing."

"What could happen? You said it yourself."

I have misgivings, but he did get the boat. I grab the beat up wooden paddle and climb in the front.

The trip starts out peaceful enough, but Ty is having a hard time steering. We keep running into the bank, especially on curves. "Could ya keep it straight?"

"I'm trying, Rob. This thing just doesn't steer. You're not doing much to help."

I am trying but the boat does seem difficult to keep on a straight line.

We pass under four spans of the highway bridge—sideways—until the boat hits a rock and then we spin around backwards.

I've had enough thrills. "Pull over. I'm driving."

"Be my guest. I'd love to see you keep it straight."

We splash to a gravel bar and trade places. "Does this tube seem to be losing air?" I press on the tube, which sinks under my hand.

Ty presses it gingerly. "Looks fine to me."

"Maybe we should have kept the pump."

We head downriver again and things are going better with me driving. "Glad we switched."

"The river's straight here, Rob."

We paddle by the Peanut Farm restaurant and people eating outside point as we go by.

"Look at the kids in a kayak!"

"That looks like fun."

"Watch out for the curve up ahead," says a lady with a knowing look in her eye.

"What do you think she meant?" Ty asks.

I shrug. "We can make it. It's not the Colorado River."

We leave the congested area and the river winds us through a spruce forest.

"Why are we over on this side?" Ty asks.

I'm trying to steer the thing but it's worse than a stubborn mule. "Just looking at what's over here."

"Old spruce trees, just like the other side."

"Shut up and keep paddling."

The speed of the creek picks up and I've got my hands full trying to steer. We bang one side of the bank and the force careens us into the middle. We do a 360.

I scream instructions. "Paddle on the other side of the boat!"

Ty listens and we make the turn.

"Can you believe it?" I kid you not, there is a full sized canoe sticking straight up out of the water, bow to the heavens, against the far side of the river as we sweep by, just missing a huge swirling eddy near a concrete culvert rushing with fresh water.

We float along, past a bike path and an area of condos. I hear rushing water ahead as we approach another bridge. "What do you see, Ty?"

"It's a little drop off. Think we can make it?"

I'm paddling frantically toward shore but we're heading right for this weird stretch of whitewater.

"Paddle right!" Ty says.

The next thing I know I'm swimming. When I surface, I see Ty in the boat without a paddle. He's gripping the edges of the boat. It's stuck in a little eddy.

The water's cold but calm again and I can stand. Ty's paddling with both hands toward shore and strangely the boat goes the right direction for once.

I walk up, teeth chattering.

"You're wet, Rob."

"I just swam the rapids." Come to think of it, Ty's looking pretty wet also. "Where are the paddles?"

The Swiss cheese paddle is washed up on the other side of the creek. The nice one is nowhere to be seen.

"Trip's over. We're up a creek without a paddle. I'm calling Mom." I reach for the cell phone. It's gone. "Must've fallen out of my pocket."

"Mom'll kill you. She's had the phone a week."

I scan the river bank. "We can make it back to the road and hitchhike." I swat at a swarm of mosquitoes that has just realized red meat is in the neighborhood.

We try to bushwhack along the river to the road but it's too thick. Lugging the boat is back-breaking.

"C'mon Rob. We can paddle with our hands to get the paddle. Plus, we need to find the other one. It's not ours. Besides, how much worse can it get?"

If I had known what was ahead, I'd have sent up smoke signals for help. Instead, I get into the kayak with Ty and we paddle with our hands and all our might to the other shore.

"Quit splashing me. I want the front."

Ty turns around. "You begged for the driver's seat."

"Keep paddling or we'll never make it."

"Make up your mind, Rob."

We actually do make it to the paddle.

"You take it, Rob. I'll guide you."

I feel like Daniel Boone paddling down a river, except that he knew what he was doing. If paddling before was hard, paddling with the holey paddle is impossible.

"Look out, Rob!" Ty ducks to avoid a tree limb that slashes across my face, leaving a track of something wet and sticky and stealing my cap.

"A little more notice would be nice."

"A little better steering would be nicer. Watch out!"

A partially submerged tree hits the boat and in an unbelievable fluke pops the air valve.

"Grab it, Ty, or we'll be deflated in minutes!"

The boat loses air at an alarming rate as we careen around a curve. Ty, scrambling to cap the valve, gets a knee on the side of the boat and we take on water. My mind wanders from Daniel Boone to the Titanic.

"I got it."

It's a miracle. He's managed to cap the valve and we're still afloat. But we've lost all navigation as the boat is as soft as a marshmallow and drives like one.

Suddenly, Ty ducks, covers his head, and emits a high-pitched scream that could wake the dead. At the same moment, a huge bundle of fur with red teeth the size of my thumbs launches itself at the kayak from the bank.

"Vampire beaver!" Ty yells, paddling with his arms and shoveling water onto the already precarious boat.

I'm stunned at the size of the retreating beaver.

"We scared the poor guy."

"Why are his teeth red? He's probably been chewing on the last guys down this accursed creek."

"Beaver don't eat meat." Do they?

"Rob, we're heading toward a tree across the river."

Sweepers are very dangerous. They can catch a boat and boaters and keep them under until they drown.

"Lean forward and paddle!"

"You've got the paddle!"

"Use your hands or whatever you've got." The half-submerged boat is like paddling a kid's swimming pool.

We don't clear the tree, but Ty grasps a branch and shoves, spinning us away from the killer.

"Yippee!" he yells, just before we're impaled on a tree limb.

We try to save her, but the current's too strong. We end up swimming to shore, completely empty handed.

As we climb out, taking one last look at the predicament of the rubber kayak, Ty bends over laughing. "You look terrible. Your hair's a bigger mess than usual, you've got a gash across your face, and your clothes are clinging to your goose bumps."

"Shut up and walk." As fortune would have it, we're on the bike path side of the creek. "I think Taku Lake is up ahead. We can borrow a phone and call Mom from there."

We slog to the lake, leaving a trail of wet shoe prints. Or three shoe prints and one footprint, since I seem to have lost a shoe.

"There's a family fishing. I'm sure they have a phone."

We trudge up, wearing our lifejackets, and suddenly my day becomes the worst day of my life.

"Excuse me," Ty starts, "could we borrow a phone to call our mom?"

A girl at the lake turns around. It's Jasmine.

Please don't recognize me. Please don't recognize me. Please don't recognize me, I pray to the heavens.

"Look Rob! It's Jasmine, from Resurrection Bay!"

Jasmine, as beautiful as ever, comes toward us and hands over her phone. "The kayak and whale guys." A smile is forming at the corners of her mouth, her gorgeous eyes sparkle.

Ty nods. "See, Rob, she remembers us."

I nod, mute. How could she not?

"How could I forget you? You two manage to always leave an impression." Her face cracks into an all out, spectacular smile showing perfect teeth.

"That means we're unforgettable, right Rob?"

"Dad'll probably give you a ride home," Jasmine offers.

I'm feeling faint. "That's okay. I'll probably die right here."

"I'll take a ride," Ty says. "You wouldn't believe what happened to us."

"Somehow," Jasmine says, "I would."

Alaska Grown

Denali Park requires all back country users to carry and store food in a thick plastic bear-proof container. If a bear goes through someone's camp, it may smell but can't eat the food so does not associate people with food.

June 25th

Started my five day backpack trip in Denali Park. By myself. My training has come in handy already. Did 10 miles today. Took the Park bus in to Polychrome Pass. Stepping off the bus with my pack and then off the gravel road was sweet. Didn't take long to leave all the people, buses and signs of civilization behind. Spent much of the day walking a gravel river bed. Had to cross the braided river several times. Freezing!

Found a great spot to put my tent, behind a boulder several stories high. How'd the freaking thing get here, anyway? Cracked open my bear canister and had a feast, of dried food cooked over my tiny stove. Haven't seen a bear yet. Tons of mosquitoes though.

They're called the Alaska state bird. Lucky someone at the Park entrance gave me a head net or I'd be one big itchy welt.

Midnight and still light. Don't know how I'll sleep. So quiet. Left my tunes at home on purpose, and phones don't work here. A California boy like me isn't used to the unnatural quiet. So quiet I want to scream.

Just did--feel better.

June 26th

Got an itinerary with the Park Service yesterday. Backcountry permits are for certain areas to limit impact. Since I came so far yesterday, decided to stay put today. Day hiked up a steep slope—no trees—just bushes and plants. Lots of flowers. Saw a grizzly munching on plants in the distance. Marmots and other animals with huge ears in the rocks. Looked sort of cuddly. Tomorrow I head to the next area. No cell service, even on the mountain. Probably won't have any the whole trip. Freaky, but trying not to think about it. Can't believe I'm out here on my own. No one for miles.

June 27th

Did about 12 miles today. Feel like I'm right in the middle of the Denali wilderness. Glad the GPS works. At least I know where I am. Climbed over a hill and along a ridge with unbelievable views. Sunny all day. Then down into a riverbed for easy walking. The brush is terrible, tearing at your legs. Ridge walking and riverbed walking easiest. Few trails in this land

and those are made by game. A moose scared the crap out of me in the riverbed just before I made camp. Heart's still racing. Thought it was a grizzly. Scared the moose worse. Thundered off at a gallop with her baby behind. Climbed a hill to set up camp to get out of the brush so I can see. Admit I feel lonely. Nothing but mosquitoes to keep me company, though fewer up here in a breeze.

June 28th

Feel lucky to be alive. Tumbled down a steep ridge today. Knocked out. When I came too felt like I'd been hit by a truck. Took some time to get my wits together. My backpack was still on but my food container must've fallen off and rolled because it's nowhere in sight. Wrenched a shoulder and had dried blood on my hands and face. No mirror to see the damage. Hope it hasn't marred my classic looks. Worst of all is my ankle, broke for sure. The pain is unbearable. Crawled to the creek nearby to wash up and drink. No energy to treat the water. Probably start puking anytime. Somehow managed to set up my tent and pass out on my bag. Now I'm starving. Wish I'd never come. Probably won't sleep tonight.

June 29th

This morning was convinced I'd die right here, the pain in my ankle was so bad. Passed out again just taking a leak. Slept until noon, then decided I better quit feeling sorry for myself. Tore a shirt into strips and cut a few short lengths of brush. Then I straightened my ankle. When I revived I tied the stays around my lower leg. Still hurts but now doesn't jostle. Feel empty with no food but loading up on water. Tomorrow will look for food. Got to. Just remembered. Today is the day I was supposed to leave the park.

June 30th

Woke to a steady rain, just to make life more fun. Made a cane from a piece of brush and hobbled or hopped around all day looking for my food canister. Never found it. Too scared to eat the vegetation but may have to or die. Shoulda bought the book on edible plants in the bookstore. Distracted by thoughts of food and every meal I've ever eaten.

July 1st

Another day of searching for food, ankle pain enough to make me puke water and bile when it touches the ground. Rain all day. Know I need to keep moving and keep drinking. Fox came by and peed all around my tent, especially where I've been peeing. Would've tried to feed him if I had food. Instead screamed and he ran away. Hollow and hopeless. Don't know if I can keep my energy up. Days drag by. I may die out here.

July 2nd

Pepperoni pizza, soda, bread sticks, ham and eggs, bacon, PB&J, bananas, fried chicken, mashed potatoes, ice-cream…

Beginning to hallucinate. Gorgeous girl walking toward me up the river bed in the pouring rain. Blond braids, rain hat and food container in her arms.

I'm pinching myself. Surely I'm dreaming.

"Michael Jamison?" the beautiful lips say, leaning to look into my tent.

"Mike." My lips feel parched and my voice cracks like I haven't spoken in weeks.

"Shelby! He's over here!" She turns back to me. "I'm Kristen, Mike. My partner Shelby and I are part of mountain rescue."

I'm speechless as another gorgeous girl approaches, this one a brunette. Both are carrying large, well-equipped packs.

Now I know what you're thinking. Brother, you're alone in the wilderness so long any babe looks sweet. But I swear these two could be models.

"You got my food?"

Kristen laughs, a sweet, bell-like sound. "Figures his first words are about food."

"I'm starving. Nothing to eat for days. Practically dead."

"You look far from dead." She sets my bear container outside the tent. "Eat up, Mike."

I grab the first edible thing and wolf it down. The girls stand and stare. "Want to come in?" I gesture inside.

"First you've got to tell us what's up. You're overdue, we've found you, and we need to radio your location."

"They're looking for me?"

"Park Service tries not to lose anyone. This part of the Park's been socked in for days. Can't get a plane or helicopter in the sky. Checked the more accessible areas for you yesterday."

I'm stunned. I can't believe this.

"He's mute. Maybe a brain injury. There's a gash on his head. I'm going in." Kristen slings off her pack, shedding rain water everywhere.

I'm not going to argue about a sexy chick visiting my pad no matter where I am. "Ankle."

Kristen pulls my pants leg up and runs her hand along my bones. "Rest of the leg looks good. He's got it splinted nicely so I think we should leave it."

Shelby nods. She pulls out a radio. "Mobile Three to Operations Base, Over."

Nothing but static. Shelby tries several times from different parts of the riverbed. "It's like a black hole for communications here. Usually these Park Service radios are good for 20 miles."

I can't take my eyes off these two and feel like I've landed in some type of altered reality. Models, actresses, co-eds, but not rescuers. Suddenly I hope we're stuck here together, alone, for a few more days.

"Probably get reception from the top of the ridge," Kristen suggests, pointing.

"Fogged in now. I'm not going up there today."

"You didn't fall down that, did you, Mike?"

I nod.

"You're lucky you weren't killed."

I'm feeling very lucky right now. Funny how fortunes change. "You can stay in my tent tonight."

Kristen laughs again. "Mike, we've got everything we need and enough for you, too."

I'm still trying to wake from this surrealistic dream. "Where are you from?"

"We live just down the road. Been doing mountain rescue for years."

Shelby has managed to light a fire out of wet wood and something from her pack. "Colder than usual this year."

"You look my age."

"Know your bio by heart. 'Michael Jamison. Solo hiking. 18 years old. Tall, dark hair, brown eyes. From Southern Cal. Left on 7/25 and due back 7/29. Says he's good with a GPS.' Sorry to tell you, Mike, but you're in the wrong back country area."

I ignore the last information. "How do you know all that?"

"We profile all missing hikers. Helps us find them, especially if we can piece together some clues. Found your first camp this morning. Boulder camp. Very popular."

I'm starting to get mad. "Really. If everything I do is so predictable why don't you just drop from the sky and lift me out of this hell hole?"

"Rescuing people is a little harder than that, Mike." Kristen leaves the tent and she and Shelby put up theirs in less than five minutes.

I miss her already. "And you all are experts."

"Some people call us so. Rescued the last missing hiker too. Have a knack for it."

"We're the park superintendent's daughters."

"Saints," I say sarcastically. "And how old are you?"

"So Cal jock is so impolite. Probably from Orange County." Kristen high fives Shelby.

I don't give them the satisfaction of knowing their guess is right. And Mickey Mouse is my best friend.

"We need to radio tonight. I think I had reception about half a mile back." Shelby's studying the radio.

"I'll go with you. Mike looks like he's doing fine."

I shrug. "My breathing seems a little shallow and my heart's racing."

"You look fine to me," Kristen says, exiting the tent. "Guys," she says to Shelby, loud enough so I can hear.

While they're gone I can't help but fantasize about them. Kristen's got a great figure, and Shelby long legs. Could be as tall as I am. Too bad they're in all that baggy raingear. They'd look great at the beach. Probably whiter than lilies and burn to a crisp in minutes. I stifle a laugh. Alaskan girls probably don't even own a bathing suit.

Finally I hear laughing and the chicks reappear.

"What took you so long?"

"Had to pick up a pizza on the way."

"Very funny."

"Chopper will be here in the morning to pick you up."

"I'm just getting used to the scenery."

Shelby ignores the comment and kneels by her pack. "Want to join us for dinner?"

"No thanks. Got my own food thanks to you." I'm trying to figure out how I'm going to relieve myself with these two around. I've got to figure it out fast.

"Moose meat stew. Kris shot and butchered it herself, then packed it home."

"Three trips to carry it all."

They're gorgeous, they rescue folks, and shoot their own food. What next? I crawl out of my tent and hobble toward a bush. Every step is agony. Next thing I know each girl's got one of my arms over her shoulder and they're carrying me to a bush. I can't believe they're strong enough to lift me.

"Weight lifting," Shelby says to my unasked question.

They set me down and go back to their business while I do mine. They reappear when I'm done.

"I can make it." Anything to save my wounded pride.

They shrug and leave me and I hop, cursing once as I make it over to their fire. The stew smells so good my mouth waters.

"Sure you don't want any?"

I'm stubborn. I don't want these girls to get the best of me. I shake my head and grab some jerky, crackers and an energy bar from my container. Shelby's dishing up the best looking camping food I've ever seen. She brings some for me, too. Must see the stream of drool running down my mouth.

The girls ignore me, which is fine because I'm wolfing down the food like I haven't eaten in weeks. They laugh and carry on as the dusk deepens. How can two chicks spend all day together and still have things to talk about late into the evening?

"I'm going to bed."

"See you in the a.m. Be packed and ready to go. The guys don't like to wait when they're hovering like that."

I think about giving the girls my e-mail address and an invite to CA for finding me. I could show them around Hollywood, go to the beach, and go out on the town.

As I'm drifting off, two flutes play a haunting counter melody. Somehow it's the nail in the coffin. These two are completely out of my league.

July 3rd

Helicopter couldn't land so they lowered a basket. 8 a.m. sharp. Shelby and Kristen half carried me to the basket. Climbed in myself. Before the basket was raised, Kristen shoved a note into my hand and a green t-shirt that said "Alaska Grown". The note said "Next time you're here we'll take you rock climbing and fishing." Then it had a phone number.

I waved to Kristen and Shelby and knew one thing. I had been outdone in every way by two chicks, probably younger than me. Alaskan chicks rock!

Bloody Extra Toughs

The Park Service rents cabins in remote areas around the State of Alaska. Users reserve the cabins on line months ahead of time for a nominal fee. Cabins are bare bones, with wooden bunks, a wooden table, an outhouse and no electricity or running water.

"They say this cabin is haunted," Tyler says, flipping pages in the log book.

"You don't believe in ghosts, do you, Ty? And in a Park Service cabin?" We've rented the cabin at Picturesque Cove in Prince William Sound for the weekend with Mom and Dad. They're out cruising in the boat while Ty and I opted to stay in. It's pouring outside and we have a Gameboy competition going.

Ty looks uncertain. "I wouldn't be surprised if a ghost or two lived here."

It is a dark cabin. Even in daylight it has a dingy look, with moss collecting on the roof and a stale stench in the air, almost like urine. "What does the book say?"

"'July 2nd. We didn't get a wink of sleep. There was a creaking and groaning in the cabin, almost as if it were alive...'"

"Wind, I'm sure."

"'...and it's not even windy tonight. There are voices. We can't make out what they're saying. In the morning, fresh drops of blood on the porch'." Ty looks at me.

"So what. Noises are explainable, and wild animals are all over the place in this thick forest."

"'July 8th. As the day progressed, a terrible odor developed like a rotting carcass or the inside of a sewer. I could think of nothing but death all night long'."

"Probably something crawled in and died under the cabin."

"'July 10th. We left for a paddle. When we got back our food was gone, except for the cans'."

"So a varmint carried it away."

Ty's eyes are wide. "What kind of varmint? Bears leave a big mess and foxes don't scavenge in cabins."

I shrug. "Those things aren't even scary, Ty."

"The guy goes on. 'I think I must be crazy, but someone's watching us. I see shadows across the window but when I look no one's there. This morning there was a bloody mess of entrails near the tide line. It was so big, I don't know what critter it was from. Next to it was an old blade that looked like it was chiseled from stone'."

"That's ridiculous. I can't believe you think this crap is true. I'm going to the outhouse." I leave, letting the door slam behind me. I see Ty jump as I walk by the window. At the outhouse, I notice something I haven't seen before. With a sharp implement, someone has scratched 'RIP Roxanne of the Ravens'. It looks weathered, but this climate is tough on everything. On the way back to the cabin I grab a dead branch, sneak up to the cabin, and run it down the uneven side. I hear running footsteps inside and the door slam. I toss the stick and saunter up to the porch.

Ty looks like he's seen the ghost of Roxanne of the Ravens. "Did you see anything?"

"No, why?"

"Nothing." Ty is freaked.

Mom and Dad arrive soon after. Ty jumps when they come through the door.

Mom laughs. "It looks like you've seen a ghost."

"Ty thinks this place is haunted."

Dad laughs. "I hope you boys don't believe in nonsense like that."

"I don't."

"I don't either," Ty parrots, but he looks relieved Mom and Dad are back.

After dinner we play poker until the lantern goes out.

Dad shakes the lantern. "That's strange. I thought this thing was full."

Mom picks it up. "Empty. Great. And two nights left. Next time I fill it."

Ty looks at me. I shrug.

"Phew! Who did that? It stinks like the dead." Mom pinches her nose and gives me and Ty a dirty look.

"Ty," I point.

"Rob," he points.

"Come on. You did it. Yours always stink."

"I swear I didn't."

"Stop it boys and get in bed."

I turn to get my bag and trip, falling flat on my face.

Dad gives me a withering look. "Quit the horseplay before someone gets hurt in this small space."

"We didn't do it!" we both say together.

Somehow we get everything sorted out and I hear gentle snoring. The smell of decay lingers in my nostril. Ty never changes his socks. I'm surprised his feet haven't rotted off and he's walking around on bloody stumps.

Sometime in the middle of the night I hear the worst grinding noise I've ever heard. The whole cabin is shaking.

"The monster will get us!" Ty yells.

Dad climbs out of bed with a flashlight. I follow him to the door. The grinding, chewing noise continues.

I admit my heart pounds as I grasp the door handle. "It sounds like it's at the door." My voice cracks.

Dad grabs the door and throws it open. A huge porcupine squints in the beam of light and scrambles off the porch. Another flees from under the cabin and they both lumber away.

"What was it?" Mom asks.

"Porcupine." I'm chagrined to hear relief in my voice.

"Chewing on the wood around the door. Should've seen the marks."

"Ty probably thought it was the teeth of the dead."

"Not funny, Rob." Ty's face is white over the top of his sleeping bag.

"It smells disgusting in here," Dad says before climbing into bed.

I don't think I've closed my eyes when the chewing sound is renewed with force. There's a scraping sound on the roof along with the sound of rain.

"Chains, a saw, a machete…" Ty intones.

I pull the sleeping bag over my head. The noise is less, but the stench is worse. Maybe it's me. I try to sleep but it's no use.

At 5 a.m. all the noises stop. The front door opens and slams shut and the floor boards of the cabin squeak as under the weight of feet.

My heart pounds as I sit bolt upright. Ty screams like a guy never should, high and eerie. Mom and Dad sit up in the early morning twilight. All are accounted for, so who opened the door?

"Who left the window open?" Dad gets up to close it.

I know you may not believe this, but I know the window was closed because I closed it during the card game. I'm feeling unnerved as I lie down. Only then do I notice the stench is gone.

I think I sleep, but maybe not. For sure my imagination is running wild. I dream a headless woman named Roxanne walks through the cabin in knee high Extra Tough gum boots, wearing nothing but seaweed, blood streaming down her torso. Her head, mouth set in a scream, is dragged behind by a chain.

Finally I hear moving in the cabin. Peeking out of my bag I see Mom and Dad, not a bloody ghost.

"That was the worst night of my life," Mom says. "Don't think I slept a wink."

"The smell alone was enough to keep a person awake. I can still taste it." Dad runs a hand through his hair, making it stick up.

"Let's leave this morning," Mom suggests.

Ty is out of his bag faster than a sprinter and shoving his sleeping bag into its stuff sack.

Dad leaves to pee. "What in heaven's name? The Zodiak's gone!"

We all hurry to the porch. Our boat is anchored serenely in the harbor and there is no sign of the landing craft.

"We're stuck!" Ty wails.

We run to the beach. Dad puts binoculars to his eyes. "I think I see it, floating free. Rob, get the marine radio."

I run inside. It's not too long before Dad hails a passing boat in Culross Passage and the guy retrieves our Zodiak, dragging it into the cove. "Bad knot, huh?" the guy says, giving Dad a knowing look.

Dad forces a laugh. "Guess so."

As the guy revs the engine and leaves us on the beach, we're unusually quiet. Dad ties off the Zodiak not once, but twice, then three times. Dad's an expert at knots. At parties he ties them blindfolded. "Get the boat loaded."

We go back into the cabin. It's only then we realize all our food is gone.

We can't get out any faster. We've never worked so well together.

I see the same relief I feel mirrored on everyone's face as the engine turns over and we see the cabin retreating in the wake of the boat.

"I had the strangest dream," Mom says. "All I remember is bloody Extra Toughs…"

"Roxanne!" Ty and I whisper together.

Avalanche

Snow machiners like to drive their machines straight up a steep slope and as they're losing speed, turn and race downhill. "High marking" leaves a perfect parabolic track on the mountainside.

"Please, Dad. Look at the perfect day." Jaz was begging, and he knew it.

"The perfect day for an avalanche," his dad replied.

Twelve inches of fresh snow late in the year, sunny, and 45 degrees. Jaz knew the recipe for avalanche risk. "You'd go if you didn't have to work."

Jaz held steady under the stern gaze of his father, who glanced at his watch. "Take the safety gear and you're back by 5:30. No high marking."

Jaz was texting a message as the door slammed. "Can do. Meet in 5."

"Three sleds loaded and ready," from Shane and Brent, the brothers next door.

Jaz threw his gear in a duffle and filled a plastic bag with food raided from the fridge. A horn blared from the driveway. Jaz ran through the garage, grabbing the two safety bags, his and his father's, as he exited into the bright sun, squinting.

"Geez, the crap you bring," Brent said, scooting toward his brother on the long bench seat.

"Dad. Avalanches and all."

Brent shrugged, opening the bag of chips Jaz handed over. "Perfect Alaskan weather. A perfect graduation present."

"Who'd've guessed after the warm weather this week," Shane said from behind his wrap around shades.

It had been a long and utterly satisfying day of sledding through the fresh but heavy snow of Turnagain Pass, marred by few other snow machine tracks. Jaz looked at his watch. 4:00. "Gotta head back," he yelled over the noise of the machines.

Brent gave a thumbs up.

"You guys look like twins in the matching jackets and helmets."

Shane shrugged. "Except I've got the safety bag and avalanche beacon. Gotta take one more run up there." He pointed up a steep slope they had passed earlier.

"Too steep," Jaz replied, remembering his dad's warning.

Shane winked under his raised visor. "It's perfect." He revved his machine and gunned it, jetting up in a perfect parabolic curve.

"Damn, he's got guts," Brent said as the two boys squinted into the sun.

Suddenly the entire side of the mountain liquefied, crumbling under the weight of Shane, his machine, and the heavy spring snow.

Jaz's heart stopped as he watched the avalanche play out as if in slow motion and Shane disappear under the massive amount of snow roaring down in front of them. It was over in seconds.

Jaz jumped off his machine and grabbed Brent as he sat frozen on his machine. "No time to waste." He sprinted to the base of the slide. He knelt, undoing his emergency pack. His avalanche beacon was on, and he knew the other beacon, which Shane carried strapped to his back, was on too.

Jaz's heart pounded as he struggled to remember his avalanche training. His shaking hands dropped the beacon in the snow. Brent looked like he was in shock. Jaz threw him the probe and shovel out of his pack. "Snap the probe together."

Jaz set his beacon to receive. "We have less than 15 minutes to locate him or he's dead." The beacon indicated nothing as Jaz began walking over the thick, clumpy snow, vaguely aware of Brent in his wake. Finally he got a reading. Forty meters, his beacon announced. Jaz kept walking in his chosen line. Fifty meters.

Jaz gave up on that line and zigzagged up the slope. Thirty meters. 25 meters. 30 meters. Jaz drifted left. 20 meters. 10 meters. "He's near here!"

Brent started digging through his tears.

"Not yet." Seven minutes had passed and Jaz

felt sweat beading on his forehead as the sun beat down. He paced and repaced a small grid. Three meters was the closest reading he got. "Probe!" Jaz grasped the 10-foot probe and began a patterned search. Within a minute he felt a resistance. A few inches away a definite hit.

"Dig here." Brent laid into the snow with all his energy. Jaz dug too, with his gloved hands. Damn, another shovel would help.

"I see him!" Brent sobbed. Shane's bright blue jacket and what could be an arm were visible. The boys redoubled their effort. "We need his head."

"Careful," Jaz cautioned Brent as the metallic sound of shovel on helmet rang in the air. Brent abandoned the shovel and both boys dug with their hands.

"Shane!"

There was no response. Jaz's watch showed 14 minutes had passed since Shane disappeared.

Shane was on his side, limbs splayed, eyes open and face pale under packed snow in and around his helmet.

"He's dead," Brent breathed, standing and then bending over and puking all over the snow.

Jaz swallowed around the gorge in his own throat as he continued to remove snow from around Shane's face.

"Help me get the helmet off and keep digging him out!"

Jaz bent close over Shane's face, feeling for a pulse with his hand. Nothing. Jaz swiped snow out of Shane's mouth. He ripped down the zipper of Shane's coat and started pounding on his chest with both hands.

"Breathe, Shane. Breathe."

Jaz breathed a few gulps of air into Shane's mouth and reassessed. Nothing.

Brent was kneeling beside Shane now and pounding on his chest. "I hate you for leaving me."

Jaz breathed again into the cold, slack lips. Sixteen minutes, his watch said. Did he see something move in Shane's face? "Stop, Brent."

Shane's body shuddered and he started to hack, water draining from his nose and mouth.

"Shane, you moron," Brent whispered, crying like an idiot.

"Hand me my coat." Jaz turned Shane on his side and stuffed the wadded coat under his head.

Now that Shane was breathing, Jaz assessed the rest of the situation. One arm was definitely broken, and an ankle angled unnaturally. Shane groaned as he moved it.

"Why isn't he talking?"

"He's shocky. We need help now."

Brent looked at his cell phone. No service. "Stupid phone." Brent threw it as far as he could up the slope.

"Get the plastic from my sled. Give me your jacket."

Brent did as he was told, looking relieved someone was taking control.

"Now lay out the plastic. Put my parka down first and let's slide him onto it." Jaz grasped Brent and Shane's matching coats, struggled with the zippers until they zipped together. Shane was shaking now. "Zip me in with him and cover us with the plastic."

Jaz wrapped his arms around his best friend. Damn, but he was like ice even with his clothes on.

"Get on your machine and ride for help. We don't have much time."

Silence descended on Jaz as the breep, breep of Brent's machine died away into the distance.

Shane's life depended on Jaz's actions. Jaz slipped his warm hands under Shane's shirt and rubbed his skin until his arms ached. He calmed Shane's thrashing limbs by holding him tight against himself.

Shane relaxed and went limp. He was still breathing but his breath was ragged.

Jaz looked at his watch. It was getting late and Brent hadn't returned. In fact, no one had come. Jaz started doubting himself. What else could he do for his friend? Maybe he should have loaded him onto a machine and driven him out. What would he do if Shane died on him, right then and there?

Jaz started talking. "Remember the night in the snow cave? Your end collapsed. You always had the luck. Or the time we took the sleds up north and got lost until the guy on the dog sled found us?"

Shane was silent, and seemed calmer. Jaz didn't know if this was a good or a bad thing. Still he kept on. "I could've killed you for stealing my prom date."

Shane stirred at that comment. "You're a terrible dancer anyway. Think you did it to spite me."

It was the longest hour of Jaz's life, until the sound of several machines interrupted his monologue.

Jaz watched as if from a distance several men working on Shane. He was vaguely aware of Brent at his side. A Life Flight helicopter landed on a flat area several hundred yards away and two male flight nurses with a stretcher came and whisked both Shane and Brent away.

Jaz was rooted to the spot. One of the rescuers approached his elbow.

"You did really well. You may have saved his life."

Jaz nodded numbly as he climbed on his machine. In his heart, though, he wondered if his best friend had died in his arms.

Never Sled with a Two Year Old

"Rob, I can still take you and Tyler sledding, but Travis will have to come too," Mom announces.

Travis the two year old terror from next door. "Mom, this is our family time," I try. "There's no way it'll be fun with Travis along."

Mom glares at me. "Listen, young man. Where's your charity and compassion? A neighbor needs help and we're going to help. We don't have to go sledding."

Tyler's behind Mom, shaking his head and gesturing wildly. I know he really wants to go. Sledding isn't just for little kids in Alaska. We've been dying to do the mile-long path through the woods at Arctic Valley since a foot of snow fell two days ago. The only problem is you need a car to take you to the top each time.

When I hesitate, Ty jumps in. "We'll take Travis. It'll be fun, won't it Rob?" He puts an arm around my shoulder and a knuckle in my ribs. I hate to admit he's grown over the summer and is about my size now and his voice has gotten deeper. I'm still better looking, though.

I nod. "We'll take good care of the tyke."

Mom looks at each of us. "He's my responsibility and he's got to be safe."

"He'll ride with Rob." "He'll ride with Ty," we say together, pointing.

"You'll take turns. The minute something goes wrong, we're heading home."

"Comprende, Mom. Seriously. It's sledding. What could go wrong?"

"After the misadventures of this summer?" Mom looks torn between outrage and laughter. Ty hangs his head. He's feeling remorse about his part in everything. Or he's trying not to laugh.

Mom shakes her head. I guess her humor wins. "You boys are something," she says, walking out the front door.

"Probably wishes she had girls," Ty says in falsetto.

I sock him. "You're a lot of help. Go get the sleds."

Minutes later we're all loaded into the Subaru, Travis in his car seat and bundled up head to toe. All I can see is cheeks and eyes under the hat, neck warmer and jacket hood. His arms stick out to the side in the quilted, red snowsuit.

I buckle in next to him. "Cute little guy." I tickle the only piece of flesh I see and he turns and bites my finger.

I pull the digit out of his mouth. "Lay off!"

"Part piranha," Ty laughs.

I pop Ty upside the head.

Mom squeals the car to a stop. "Absolutely no violence in the car. The roads here are treacherous enough."

I cross my arms and sulk. This day isn't turning out as planned. I swear Travis understands and gives me a knowing look. "Shape up, Buster, or we miss sledding," his eyes say.

I am a model of good behavior as Mom winds up the steep road to the start of the run. At the top, we pile out. Ty gets the sleds as I unhook Travis from the car seat. "Keep your teeth to yourself," I say under my breath. No joke, the kid clacks them together. "Thank God you don't talk yet." So far, he's been mute.

I set Travis down, grasping the gloved hand, as we wave good-bye to Mom.

"You get him first," I say to Ty.

"Where is he?"

I look down. All I've got is the glove. "He was just here."

We see a flash of red as Travis, teetering on the edge, belly-flops to the snow and starts careening downward, yelling "No, No, No!"

Ty and I grab our sleds and take off after him. Travis the Torpedo is well ahead. "We've got to catch him before Dead Man's Curve."

Ty looks frantic. "I think he's scared, Rob. He's yelling 'No'. I can still hear it. Poor kid."

"Mom's going to kill us." The run's a little icy and I whiz past Ty. I think I'm gaining on Travis. The big curve is coming up.

"Slow down, Rob!"

I try to steer and the sled flips. My belly tightens as I twist in mid-air and let out a "whump" as I hit the ground hard.

Ty halts his sled. "That was awesome! Are you okay?"

"Get the kid." I manage to roll onto my sled and follow, spitting out globs of snow. Soon I see Ty's purple sled off to the side. I stop. Ty's peering into the woods.

"He made the curve, got to here, and now he's off and running."

I can just see a blur of red under the gloom of trees ahead. "Mom's really gonna kill us if we lose him."

Ty and I look at each other for a split second and then dash into the trees.

The snow is deep and we wallow through it in pursuit. Travis is so light he walks on top. He's got another advantage, too. He's short. I push spruce branches out of my way, but still they poke at my face and tear at my clothes. Finally Ty grabs the Terror. "Gotcha!"

Travis is laughing his head off. "He's clean as a whistle, like he just got out of the car," Ty says. "You on the other hand, are covered."

"'No ball," Travis says, pointing at me.

Soon Ty and Travis are both laughing. "He does look like a snowball. Or a snowman."

I pick some cling-on icy chunks off. "Very funny."

"You've got spruce twigs and moss in your hair. Where's your hat?"

"Some tree's wearing it." I stalk off, never finding the hat.

I'm just getting to the sleds when Travis Terrific bombs past me, yelling "'No! 'No! 'No!'" and lands in a sled before I can grab him.

"Why'd you let him go?" I yell at Ty as we both climb onto the remaining sled.

"He was behaving himself and getting heavy."

"After him!" I point to Travis, who's going downhill backward.

With both of us in it, the sled flies downhill like it has wings. Ty tries to steer on the right and we turn the wrong way, get sideways and flip, rolling over and over. Lying on the snow we watch as the sled rights itself and nose downward, leaves us in the dust.

We have no choice but to catch Travis on the run. Ty's ahead of me as Travis takes to the air and lands in a huge drift.

Ty pulls him out and the kid is actually laughing. "'No! 'No! 'No!"

"I've had enough for one day." Every bone in my body aches. "Keep your hands on the kid. He's an escape artist." I right the sled and it's a tight fit, me, Ty, and Travis on his lap. "'No! 'No! 'No!" Travis yells.

"The word is 'snow', kid. S-now."

Great. Ty's a speech therapist now.

"I'll steer. You keep your hands on Travis."

"Right, boss, but we're heading toward the mogul section at the end."

I don't know why, whether it's the wind or what, but every year there's a carved up section of bumps at the end of the run. I try to slow down, but soon we're taking air.

"Snow!" Whump. "Snow!" Whump. "Snow!" Travis yells.

I can't believe we're actually still in the sled as I see the road ahead. The final mogul gets us. The last thing I see as we wipe out is the red blur of a snowsuit flying over my head.

"No!" Ty yells.

"Snow!" Travis yells.

I'm flat on my back for the third time, trying to bring air into my flattened lungs.

Tyler's laughing. I sit up and Travis is in a tree, hanging by his suit.

"Snow!" he says.

Ty unhooks him and we approach the parking lot. Both sleds are in front of the car. At least they have some sense.

"Want to go again?" Mom asks as I crawl into the back seat.

"No! No! No!" is all I can muster.